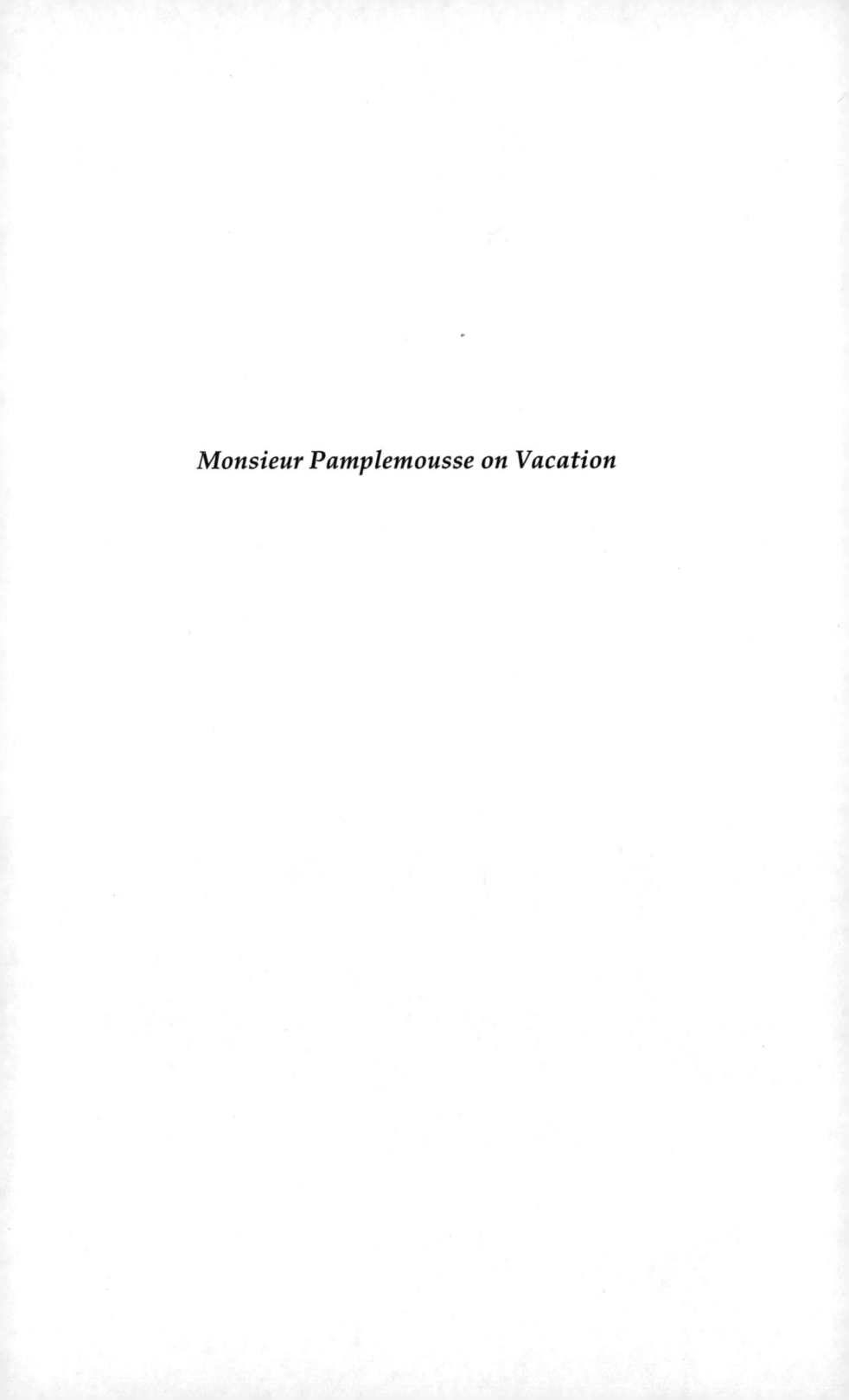

Monsieur Pamplemousse on Vacation

Monsieur Pamplemousse

on Vacation

MICHAEL BOND

First published in Great Britain in 2002 by
Allison & Busby Limited
Suite 111, Bon Marche Centre
241-251 Ferndale Road
Brixton, London SW9 8BJ
http://www.allisonandbusby.ltd.uk

Copyright © 2001 by MICHAEL BOND

The right of Michael Bond to be identified as
author of this work has been asserted by him in
accordance with the Copyright, Designs and
Patents Act, 1988

This book is sold subject to the condition that it shall not,
by way of trade or otherwise, be lent, resold, hired out or
otherwise circulated without the publisher's prior
written consent in any form of binding or cover other than
that in which it is published and without a similar condition
including this condition being imposed upon the subsequent
purchaser.

A catalogue record for this book is available from the British Library

ISBN 0 7490 0532 7

Printed and bound in Spain by
Liberdúplex, s. l. Barcelona

MICHAEL BOND is the author of the series of childrens books which feature Paddington Bear. Monsieur Pamplemousse and his faithful bloodhound, Pommes Frites, made their first appearance in 1983.

There's no business like show business

'Statistically,' said Madame Pamplemousse, 'there can't be many people who travel all the way from Paris to the Côte d'Azur, only to end up being forced to watch a class of mixed infants give a performance of West Side Story.'

Monsieur Pamplemousse looked gloomily around the school hall. Statistically, as far as he could judge, they were the only ones; certainly there was no one he recognised from the train journey down.

'These things happen, Couscous,' he said.

'They do to you,' said Madame Pamplemouse, with a sigh. 'They don't to other people. Other people would be having their dinner by now.'

Doucette was quite right, of course, and there was no point in arguing. He only had himself to blame for waxing lyrical about the Hôtel au Soleil d'Or, and how lucky they were to be staying there on the Antibes peninsula at someone else's expense. In particular, he had lavished so much praise on the joy of sitting on the hotel's world famous terrace of an evening, sipping an apèritif while studying the menu as the sun slowly disappeared over the western horizon, anything less had to be an anti-climax.

And less was what they had ended up with. His employer, Monsieur Henri Leclercq, Director of Le Guide, France's oldest gastronomic bible, had seen to that. For the time being at least, it was a case of grin and bear it.

Glancing down at the mimeographed sheet of paper they had been given before the start of the show, Monsieur Pamplemousse's heart sank still further. According to a note at the bottom it wasn't due to end for another two hours. Admittedly that included a fifteen-minute interval, but from the way things were going they would be lucky if they saw the sun rise again the following morning. He decided not to mention it. At least the music was up-beat.

The twenty strong orchestra, made up mostly of girls from the senior school, was specially augmented in the percussion section by pupils from the junior forms manning triangles and tambourines.

'It's nice that everyone has a chance to take part,' said Doucette reluctantly.

Monsieur Pamplemousse gazed at his wife.

Speaking for himself, he had a sneaking suspicion that some of the smaller ones had only got the job because they had failed their auditions for any other kind of work, including that of scene shifting.

Who would be a teacher?

To be fair, the fact that so far the singing had failed to match up to his L.P. of the original cast recording was hardly surprising. Ill-equipped as they were for "finger snapping", the Jets' arrival on the scene during the opening routine set the tone for much that was to follow. The number describing the delights awaiting newly arrived immigrants to America only came near to meriting the phrase "show-stopping" when one of the more enthusiastic of the minuscule dancers overshot his mark and narrowly missed colliding with a Shark who was waiting in the wings to make an entrance.

Given the speed at which he was travelling, the fact that he failed to pass straight through the bass drum as he took a header into the orchestra was little short of a miracle.

Buddy Rich in his heyday would have been hard put to equal the cacophony of sound which rose, first from the percussion section, then from the main body of the orchestra.

For a moment or two chaos reigned. Tears cascaded down the cheeks of the infant in charge of the triangle as it was wrested from her tiny grasp. The harpist, her eyes closed in musical ecstasy, spent several seconds plucking the empty air before realising that her instrument was lying on its side, while the shrieks and squeals which rose from the string section rivalled that of the Sabine women as they met their fate.

At least there were no broken bones, but what Leonard

Bernstein would have said about it all was best left to the imagination.

'Do we have to stay, Aristide?' whispered Doucette.

'Only until the interval,' hissed Monsieur Pamplemousse.

'Pommes Frites will be wondering what has happened to us.'

'I am sure he has better things to do,' replied Monsieur Pamplemousse. 'Besides, we can hardly invite him in. He would find it very hard not to take sides. I hate to think what might happen to some of the Sharks.'

'All the same,' Madame Pamplemousse wasn't going down without a fight, 'I really don't see why we have to meet this man – this so called "art dealer" – here of all places instead of in his gallery. *If* he has a gallery.'

Monsieur Pamplemousse allowed himself a sigh. 'My dear Couscous, we mustn't look a gift horse in the mouth. You should know by now that if there are two solutions to a problem, one of which is simple and the other complicated, Monsieur Leclercq always goes for the second. It is as inevitable as the fact that night follows day. That is the way his mind works and there is no changing it.'

'Even when it is totally unnecessary, since we plan to visit Nice while we are here anyway?' persisted Doucette.

'Especially when it is totally unnecessary. He would not be happy otherwise.'

Having delivered himself of the homily, Monsieur Pamplemousse rearranged himself as best he could on a seat which would have been barely adequate for one of the cast, let alone anyone of above average bulk.

Despite his words, he couldn't help feeling uneasy. Had he been asked to write about the many missions he had carried out on the Director's behalf since he first began working for Le Guide, it would have run to several volumes. Indexing them, trying to find explanations as to when and how various events seemingly unrelated to each other became inextricably entwined, would be something else again. Footnotes would abound. Cross-references would have demanded yet another volume to themselves.

Their present situation was a case in point.

It had all begun with an evening spent with Monsieur and Madame Leclercq at their home near Versailles.

From time to time the Director and his wife took it into their heads to invite those who worked in the field, the Inspectors – who were, after all, the backbone of the Le Guide's whole operation – to dine with them. It was a form of bonding: almost the direct opposite of the American habit of allowing junior staff the privilege of wearing casual clothes to the office on a Friday, since it was a case of dressing up rather than dressing down.

That apart, given the surroundings; the beautifully tonsured lawns, the immaculate gardens, not to mention the food and the wine, few would have wished to forgo the pleasure. Only the wives had reservations, for in their case it inevitably meant an extra visit to the hairdresser on the day and as the moment drew near long heart-searching over what to wear.

It was after dinner, when Madame Leclercq and Doucette had retired to another part of the house to talk about whatever it was ladies talked about on such occasions, that Monsieur Leclercq first broached the subject of a holiday in the South of France.

As soon as Monsieur Pamplemousse saw the bottle of Roullet *Très Rare Hors d'Age* cognac appear he knew something special was afoot. However, by then he was overflowing with the good things of life and in a benevolent mood; his critical faculties on hold for the time being, his guard lowered.

The Director chose the moment of pouring, when he had his back to Monsieur Pamplemousse, to strike.

'Is everything well with you, Aristide?' he asked casually. 'It may be my imagination or perhaps even a trick of the light, but it struck me earlier on this evening that you were not your usual self.'

Monsieur Pamplemousse, who until that moment had been feeling particularly at peace with the world, suffered a temporary relapse. He took a grip of himself. Two could play at that game.

'It has been a busy twelve months, *Monsieur*, what with one thing and another.

'There was the time I spent on the Canal de Bourgogne and the unfortunate business with your wife's Aunt. Admittedly her brother was in a sense once removed, having lived for most of his life in America… Well, given the fact that he was shot, I suppose you could say that in the end he was twice removed…but as things turned out it was scarcely a holiday…'

'Ah, yes.' The Director made haste to pass one of the large Riedel balloon shaped glasses; filled, Monsieur Pamplemousse noticed, with rather more of the amber liquid than he would have wished given all that had gone before. The Director wasn't one to stint his guests. Meursault with the *goujons* of sole, Chateau Cos d'Estournel with the pigeon and cheese, Barsac with the peaches and cream. He would have to watch his driving on the way home.

'Then,' he continued remorselessly, 'there was the time earlier in the year when you had me pick up a car in Paris – the Renault Twingo you were giving to the illegitimate grand-daughter of our late lamented Founder – and drive it down to the Auvergne. Again, if you remember, a homemade bomb planted in the boot wrecked my hotel room and very nearly took me with it… Hardly what one might call all in a day's work.'

The Director seized on the mention of Monsieur Hippolyte Duval, founder of Le Guide, to raise his glass in silent homage and effectively cut short Monsieur Pamplemousse's soliloquy.

Cupping it in his hands to warm the contents, he inhaled the vapour it gave off, then gave a deep sigh. 'Aaah! It is no wonder they call it "The angel's share."

'I know I have yet to thank you properly for all you did in both instances,' he continued, 'and on previous occasions too; but mention of them gives me the opportunity to make amends. All work and no play makes Jacques a dull boy and I think the moment has come when you should both indulge yourselves by investing in some quality time.'

The use of the Americanism confirmed Monsieur Pamplemousse's suspicions that the Director had being paying yet another visit to the New World; he usually returned armed with a supply of the latest expressions. He also noted the sudden use of the plural tense.

'My car is overdue for its first 300,000 km service,' he said dubiously. 'Since Citroen stopped making the *Deux Chevaux*, parts are often hard to come by. Doucette and I have been thinking of taking the train to Le Touquet and spending a few days with a distant cousin of hers.'

Monsieur Leclercq emitted a series of clucking noises, as though experiencing a momentary seizure. 'I was picturing somewhere rather more exotic, Pamplemousse. Somewhere further south; on the shores of the Mediterranean, *par exemple*. A spell in the sun will do you both the world of good.'

'Le Touquet can be very invigorating in June,' said Monsieur Pamplemousse, 'particularly when the wind is from the north-east, but if you get down to the beach early in the morning and find a suitable sand dune to shelter behind, there are the sand yachts to watch…provided *les Allemandes* haven't got there first…just lately Doucette has been suffering with her back…'

'In that case,' said the Director, 'a week sitting on the beach in Le Touquet will probably do her more harm than good.'

'I have been studying Shiatsu recently,' persisted Monsieur Pamplemousse. 'It is an ancient Japanese art where you apply pressure with your thumbs to various parts of the body…'

'If you do that kind of thing behind the dunes, Pamplemousse,' said Monsieur Leclercq severely, 'you may find yourself in trouble with the beach patrols.'

Draining his glass with a flourish to show that to all intents and purposes the matter was no longer up for discussion, his voice softened. 'Neither Chantal nor I will take "no" for an answer, Aristide. I will have my secretary book three seats to Nice on the TGV – *Première Classe* – no doubt Pommes Frites will wish to accompany you both.

'It is our way of saying *"merci beaucoup"*. Please do not deprive us of the pleasure.' Normally Monsieur Pamplemousse would have bided his time, waiting for some kind of catch to emerge. It always made him feel uneasy when the Director addressed him by his first name. But despite everything, the words had been spoken with such simplicity, such innocence, humility even – a quality he rarely associated with the Director – he found himself wavering.

'If that is what you really wish, *Monsieur...*'

'It is, Aristide. It is. And I know Chantal will be especially pleased.'

And on that note the evening had come to an end.

They were barely out of the front drive and heading for home when Doucette broke the news. 'Isn't it wonderful, Aristide? Madame Leclercq has been telling me all about it. And really, all they want in return is that we should pick up a piece of artwork for them. Apparently it is too precious to be entrusted to a carrier. All the same, it seems so little in return for so much. Mind you, knowing the Director I'm sure it won't all come out of his own pocket.'

Monsieur Pamplemousse resisted the temptation to say he would be surprised if any of it did, but Doucette had been so excited at the thought of an unexpected holiday he hadn't the heart to throw cold water on it. Anyway the die had been cast and the whole thing sounded innocent enough.

So what was new? Wasn't that the way most of his adventures on the Director's behalf had started?

For the same reason it came as no great surprise when at

the last minute the arrangements had been changed; picking up the painting or whatever it was at the concert rather than from the gallery itself.

As order was at last restored and the orchestra took their places and began tuning up again he glanced around the hall. Apart from the seating, it really was the most luxuriously equipped school he had ever come across.

'Not like it was in our day, Aristide,' whispered Doucette, reading his thoughts.

Monsieur Pamplemousse couldn't help thinking it wasn't like it had been in anyone's day.

As for the technical equipment… On the way in they had passed a state-of-the-art sound mixing console, the sole purpose of which seemed to be that of achieving a balance between the orchestra and the individual soloists, all of whom were equipped with concealed radio microphones. Video cameras were dotted around, set to record every moment of the production. According to the programme, edited tapes of the complete show would be available at a future date. As for the lighting rig: apart from the footlights, there were spots and fillers galore over the stage area. Suspended from bars which could be raised and lowered by remote control from somewhere behind the scenes, they wouldn't have looked out of place in a television studio. He wondered where all the money had come from.

What was it the hotel concierge had said? 'It is the only mixed infants school in France with an eighteen hole golf course.' It had sounded like a local joke at the time.

It seemed that everyone, apart from the builders, had profited from the largesse bestowed on it by some unknown Russian benefactors. The contractors had been screwed into the ground and in the end had gone bankrupt along with the architect, having had to pay out a vast sum for failing to meet the completion date. Rumour had it that almost immediately afterwards the same company had set up under another name further along the coast constructing a vast multi-story car park, but not before having been suitably recompensed for their previous loss.

It struck Monsieur Pamplemousse there might have been more to the story, but a party of Americans had come along wanting to know where the action was of an evening and caginess had set in, so he had been unable to pursue the subject.

He resolved to claim the rest of his hundred francs worth of information later.

He stole a glance at the programme. It couldn't be long before the interval. The scene had already changed to a bridal shop and Maria's first solo number.

If he had been asked to single out a possible contender for future non-stardom, he would have opted for the infant who had been chosen for the part. Her rendering of the song "I feel pretty" was a triumph of imagination over reality. The only mercy was that she made no attempt to play the large musical instrument she had round her neck. Monsieur Pamplemousse couldn't help reflecting that her father must have made a sizeable contribution to the school's facilities; a science lab, pehaps, or a new gymnasium at the very least: perhaps even the air-conditioned hall itself.

'I don't remember there being a Balalaika in the original version, do you Aristide?' whispered Doucette.

Monsieur Pamplemousse shook his head as he looked up the child's name on his sheet: "Olga Mugorvski." It sounded like a disease.

Joining in the dutiful applause at the end of her number, he fell to wondering why it was that different nationalities were often so instantly recognisable. Without even knowing the child's name he would have put her down as being Russian, or at least of Baltic extraction. It was the same with the Americans and the British; Italians and Germans too. It wasn't simply a matter of features; the cheekbones, the shape of the nose or the mouth, or even the way people dressed. It had to do with many things: their bearing for a start; the way they looked at you; the way their hair grew, and even more importantly, the way it was cut. With some there was a whole history writ large. There was the openness of people from the American mid-west: with Russians it was possible to detect a life-time of suffering in the lined faces of the old.

The young mistress who was directing the orchestra was a case in point. Dark, slender and vivacious; she couldn't possibly have been anything but French. She would have made a wonderful Maria. There was a virginal quality about her snow-white *doudounes*. During a spirited rendering of "Gee, Officer Krupke!" they threatened to burst forth each time she lifted her arms in order to signal various musical high points. It was safe to say that not a father in the audience remained unmoved. Hopes having been raised along with the arms, breaths were held, but to no avail.

Rapturous applause greeted the end of the number and cries of *encore* filled the hall. When the lights came up to signal the interval and it became clear that many a dream would remain unfulfilled, those nearest the back made a bee-line for the ticket desk to put their names down for the video.

'Wonderful, weren't they?' whispered Doucette.

'Heavenly,' agreed Monsieur Pamplemousse. 'Round and firm, yet not lacking movement when the moment was ripe, as in the final crescendo.'

'Aristide! I was referring to the children.'

Monsieur Pamplemousse stared at his wife. Truly, however many years two people spent together, there were moments when communication remained at a very primitive level. And if that were the case when discussing a matching pair of innocent *doudounes* – which possibly, although perhaps in this day and age not necessarily, remained as yet untouched by any human hand other than her own, what hope was there for the rest of mankind? Heads of State conferring over such complicated matters as the disposal of nuclear weapons would have their work cut out.

'*And* she wasn't wearing a brassiere.' Clearly, as far as

Doucette was concerned that was the end of the matter. Her copybook had been irredeemably blotted.

Monsieur Pamplemousse knew better than to argue. In any case the general hub-bub as those around them stood up to stretch their legs put an end to further conversation.

Leading the way to the back of the hall, he hovered near the entrance, half expecting to receive a tap on the shoulder, or at the very least catch sight of someone carrying a large parcel, but he looked in vain.

'Perhaps he is waiting for us in the hotel,' said Doucette, as the minutes ticked by.

Monsieur Pamplemousse gave a grunt as they turned to go back inside. 'That's not what the concierge told me. The message was very specific. Besides, he would have given us the tickets if…' He broke off at the approach of a small figure, a tray rather than a balalaika suspended from its neck.

'*Pragráma. Souvenir Programsk.*' You could have cut the accent with a knife.

Seen from close to, the child looking even more unprepossessing than she had on stage. Not so much a mixed infant as a mixed-up one. He wondered what she would become when she grew up. A tram driver, perhaps? Or a crane operator? If it were the former he wouldn't fancy the chances of anyone running for the last one back to the depot late at night.

Ignoring a bowl filled with large denomination notes held in place by a paperweight, he took one of the programmes and felt for some small change.

'*Nyet!*' The child shook its head and held up four pudgy fingers and a thumb. '*Cinq cent francs.* Fife hundreds of francs. Eet is for good cause. Eet is in aid of school library.'

Monsieur Pamplemousse froze, then slowly withdrew his hand from a trouser pocket.

'*Nyet pour vous aussi!*' he said, with feeling.

'Aristide!' Doucette looked shocked. 'She is only small.'

'She may be small,' said Monsieur Pamplemousse, 'but I

am not in the market for purchasing a deluxe edition of the complete works of Alexander Dumas.'

He could feel the child's eyes boring into him as she made her way round the room and joined a small group standing at the far side of the lobby. He guessed it must be her parents: the woman, *très solide*, with tightly-permed hair, was how he imagined the daughter would be in thirty years time. As for the father; he was definitely one of the old guard; short, barrel-chested, far removed from the current breed of slim, Armani-clad Westernised executives. Apart from the open-necked shirt and gold chain, he could have passed for a Nikita Khrushchev lookalike. The top of his shaven skull looked like an old warhead from an Exocet missile, and was probably twice as dangerous. Better a face to face meeting than have it trained on him while his back was turned.

Following a brief conversation, they all turned. The girl pointed towards Monsieur Pamplemousse. The father nodded, then patted her head affectionately before sending her on her way. None of which would have worried him overmuch if she hadn't made a throat-cutting gesture with her free hand as she left. It caused hearty laughter all round. Her father passed a comment to another man, who responded with a smile that was rendered even more mechanical by what appeared to be a row of steel teeth. In all, it could only have lasted a half a minute or so, but he was left with the distinct feeling that he hadn't heard the last of the matter. He hoped the daughter didn't have a birthday coming up.

'I didn't like the first one's ears,' said Doucette, reading his thoughts.

'And I don't like tiny tots who go around demanding money with menaces,' growled Monsieur Pamplemousse. Nor, he might have added, did he like ones that smelled strongly of pot, but then she wasn't the only one. Looking around he decided he might just as well be in Leningrad or Vladivostok. He felt an alien in his own country.

'You can tell a lot from ears,' said Doucette darkly. 'That

man's are much too small. They look as though they were stuck on as an afterthought.'

It was true. Since he had left the force, ears had become the subject of a great deal of scientific study. Prints taken from windows and doors often yielded as much, or more information than fingerprints. On the other hand, he wouldn't want to try taking the Russian's ear-prints with an inkpad.

'Shall we go?' asked Doucette, as the audience began drifting back to their seats. 'It doesn't look as though he's coming, and I really can't stand much more.'

'If that is what you would like, Couscous,' said Monsieur Pamplemousse, hoping she wouldn't choose to argue the point.

Outside, it was like walking into an oven; much as it had been when they stepped off the train that afternoon. The air was heavy with the sensuous smell of mimosa and bougainvillaea. Pommes Frites came bounding out from behind an ancient olive tree, pleased to see them as ever. If he was surprised to find them leaving when everyone else was going in the opposite direction he showed no sign, rather the reverse. Monsieur Pamplemousse registered the fact that his brows were knitted, and his eyes, or what little could be seen of them beneath large folds of flesh, looked slightly glazed; sure signs that he had been thinking. Of what, would only be revealed in the fullness of time, if then.

In truth, had he been taxed on the point, Pommes Frites would have had to admit he wasn't too sure himself, although a brain scan might well have revealed an unusual number of local disturbances in the overall pattern of his thought processes. In fact there were so many undercurrents darting hither and thither he might well have been asked to make a further appointment, for it was really a matter of sorting them into some kind of logical order.

His master's prophesy on the way down that there would be new smells for him to smell and new trails for him to follow had proved all too true, although in the end both had come to an abrupt end in the car park. Putting two and two together had led him to one inescapable conclusion. The person responsible had gone off in a car OR – and this was where confusion began to set in – had been *driven* off. And if that were the case, then it must have been in the boot rather than at the wheel.

It was for such powers of reasoning that Pommes Frites had been awarded the Pierre Armand Golden Bone Trophy for being Sniffer Dog of the Year in the days when he, too, had been a member of the Paris Sûreté.

'It was a funny evening, didn't you think?' said Doucette. 'I don't want to keep on about it, but I still can't understand why we were supposed to meet up at a school concert instead of in Nice.'

'Ours is not to reason why,' said Monsieur Pamplemousse. He watched as Pommes Frites disappeared into a clump of pine trees in order to investigate the sound of cicadas in a deserted *boules* area, the sodium lights casting a ghostly shadow as he dashed back and forth sniffing the ground. 'I'm sure he had his reasons. Perhaps he didn't want us to go to his shop.'

'In that case, why didn't he turn up?' said Doucette. 'Seeing all those Russians makes me wonder. I'll say one thing for them. They all had lovely shoes. You could see your face in them. It reminded me of the time I gave your new slippers to the Victims of Chernoble Disaster Fund. You were cross with me because you said it would be a miracle if they ever got that far. You said they were probably already being worn by some fat member of the Russian Mafiya toasting his feet in front of a roaring fire in his *dacha*.'

'It is not quite the same thing, Couscous,' said Monsieur Pamplemousse mildly.

'We don't even know how big a painting it is,' said Doucette. 'Perhaps that's why Monsieur Leclercq wanted us to go by train. Have you thought of that?'

Monsieur Pamplemousse had to admit the answer was "no". Trust a woman to home in on details.

Beyond the pine trees they passed a row of shops he didn't remember being there the last time he had visited the area: a couple of boutiques, a photographic shop and another with drawn blinds.

Pommes Frites caught up with them as they drew near the hotel, then ran on ahead and pushed his way through the revolving door.

The Concierge was nowhere to be seen and his number two rushed out from behind the counter as an errant tail made furious contact with an ancient dinner gong positioned near the lift. Other staff materialised within moments. An elderly women, her hair in curlers, appeared on the stairs.

'It used to be the fire alarm, *Monsieur*,' said the man reprovingly.

Monsieur Pamplemousse reached for his wallet. 'It is good to know it still works,' he said cheerfully. 'So often these things are mere token gestures. I must congratulate the management on keeping it as a stand-by. You never know when it may come in useful.'

Returning to his station the man reached for their room key. 'The young *Monsieur* is staying here?' he asked. 'Because, if so…'

'He has his own inflatable kennel,' said Monsieur Pamplemousse. 'I have made the necessary arrangements with the beach attendant. I will take him down there in a moment.'

'I will see that a bowl of water is made available for him before he retires for the night, *Monsieur*. Still or sparkling?'

'Still, *s'il vous plaît*' said Monsieur Pamplemousse. 'Evian.'

Having made a note, the deputy concierge preceded them to the lift, opened the doors, stood back to allow Pommes Frites entry after his master and mistress, then pressed a button for the third floor.

'It's a wonder he didn't ask what *journal* he likes in the morning,' said Doucette, as the doors slid shut. 'Or *journaux*.'

'He will go far,' said Monsieur Pamplemousse. 'Good hotel concierges are worth their weight in gold. Their importance cannot be over-estimated. For the regular visitor they provide a sense of continuity; of timelessness in an ever-changing world. For those in search of information they have no equal. I must make a note.'

'More work,' sighed Doucette. 'I thought this was meant to be a holiday.'

'When it comes to hotels and restaurants,' said Monsieur Pamplemousse, as the lift came to a halt and the doors slid open, 'there is no such thing as a holiday. The Director will still expect a report. Besides, I have a new lap-top to test. It is one of the latest models – on the cutting edge of computer design.'

'I would have expected nothing less from Monsieur Leclercq,' said Doucette.

Monsieur Pamplemousse wondered if he detected a note of irony in her voice, but she was already gazing at her reflection in the dressing table mirror. Women always had so many things to do before performing even the simplest of tasks, like going downstairs to dinner.

His colleague Bernard was fond of saying that his wife even applied fresh make-up before ringing up the butchers to make a complaint.

The terrace was crowded when they arrived back downstairs. All the prime tables nearest the sea had either been taken or had a reserved notice on them, and they were seated in a corner near the bar.

'It is more romantic,' whispered the female sommelier by way of consolation as she lit a candle for them. Any complaints Monsieur Pamplemousse might have harboured melted away.

Pommes Frites curled up under the table, his head resting between his two front paws, looked as though his mind was millions of kilometres away on another planet.

Dressed in the clothes he had worn to the concert,

Monsieur Pamplemousse felt lost without the notebook he normally kept hidden in a pocket of his right trouser leg. Reduced to relying on his memory, he fell silent while he concentrated on the food. Doucette seemed to catch the mood too and tired after their long journey, they retired to their room as soon as the meal was over, foregoing their usual *café* in case it kept them awake.

Before he went to bed, Monsieur Pamplemousse took one last look over the balcony at the scene below. The hum of conversation was a polyglot mixture of French, German, English, Japanese, plus a sprinkling of American voices.

In the distance he could see the twinkling lights of the coast road. An aeroplane drifting low overhead, lost height and its landing lights came on as it headed towards Nice airport. Over it all the sound of a piano drifted up from the bar; recalling the days of Scott Fitzgerald and Zelda, whose photographs still graced the walls. He wondered whether it merited an ear plug – Le Guide's symbol for background music, and decided not. From the medley of tunes he picked out Noel Coward's "Room With a View" and Cole Porter's "Night and Day". There was a selection of Maurice Chevalier hits. It was really very pleasant.

In the time it had taken them to come up in the lift more people had arrived. Their own table had been cleared and reset, and one of the larger reserved tables overlooking the sea was now occupied by the Russian group he had encountered at the school. Seen from on high with the moonlight shining on it, the father's head looked more like a tiny *Anglaise* Millennium Dome than a warhead.

He wondered what mysteries it might contain and if the family were just passing through or staying in the hotel. Probably the latter, since there was no sign of the daughter. Very likely she was sitting up in bed stuffing herself with whatever Russian children stuffed themselves with when they played "midnight feasts". In her case it would be a packet of something pretty solid; dried sturgeon on a stick perhaps, with a large bowl of vodka-flavoured ice-cream to follow. With luck it might make her sick.

The sommelier materialised with a bottle and presented it to the father, who nodded his approval, as well he might. Even from two floors up Monsieur Pamplemousse recognised the distinctive label with its host of brightly coloured bubbles.

It was a Côte Rotie *La Turque* from Guigal. Tasting dispensed with, the girl disappeared, returning a few minutes later with a second bottle. At anything up to 2000 francs a go, they were certainly pushing the boat out. The concierge was right about where all the money came from in that part of the world.

'Are the people who were at the table behind ours still there?' called Doucette.

Monsieur Pamplemousse leaned precariously over the edge of the balustrade.

Once again there was the ubiquitous smell of bougainvillaea. 'I think not . . . '

'There were three of them – an American and another couple. The American caught my eye because he reminded me of Tino Valentino. Remember . . . he was singing at the dance you took me to at the *Mairie* last Christmas. He was much shorter than I expected.'

'Those sort of people often are,' said Monsieur Pamplemousse, his mind on other things. 'Remember Tino Rossi?'

'The woman was definitely English, or I suppose she may have been Scottish – she had that sort of skin. She reminded me a bit of that American film star we used to go and see years ago – Greer Garson. I'm not sure what nationality her husband was. He kept looking at you. Once or twice I thought he was going to come across.'

'You should have said.' It was the story of his life. Where Doucette was concerned the action was always behind him.

'I had a feeling it might mean more work for you and we

are here on holiday. I think he may have been English too. He knew enough to raise his thumb when he was ordering. Not like so many foreigners who use their forefinger and then wonder why they get two of everything. But then at the end of the meal he left his fork with the tines pointing upwards. It was the kind of mistake that must have happened a lot in wartime. It's the little things that give you away.'

'You would have made a very good detective, Couscous,' said Monsieur Pamplemousse.

'Do you really think so?' Doucette sounded pleased as she turned off her bedside light. She gave a yawn. 'I haven't lived with you all these years for nothing.'

Monsieur Pamplemousse was about to turn back into the room when his attention was caught by a movement at the far end of a long jetty to the right of the hotel.

A fishing boat had appeared out of the inky blackness of the bay and was tying up at the end of the jetty. It rocked violently as two shadowy figures struggled to land their catch. He smiled to himself as he caught sight of Pommes Frites hurrying towards it to see what was going on. He wished he had his energy.

'Would you like me to lower the shutters, *Couscous*?' he called.'

But in the words of the famous Scottish poet, Sir Walter Scott, "Answer came there none." Doucette was already fast asleep.

It wasn't long before Monsieur Pamplemousse was in the same blissfully happy state. His last waking memory was that of hearing a series of three distant howls. Long drawn-out and mournful, they were reminiscent of the wailing of North American train crossing the prairie at night. Or so it always seemed to be in Westerns.

Had he been in a slightly less comatose state, he would undoubtedly have recognised it for what it was: the plaintive cry of a frustrated bloodhound making his way homeward to an inflatable kennel.

Though the first was man-made, and the other reflected nature in the raw, they both performed a similar function.

As Pommes Frites settled himself down for the night, he had the satisfaction of knowing that while he might not have brought his master running, at least as far as those on the terrace of the Hôtel au Soleil d'Or were concerned, they couldn't say they hadn't been warned.

Breakfast on the beach

The day had started well enough. Perhaps, on reflection, a little too well. The high note which had been struck early on would have been hard enough to sustain under any circumstances. But after the football landed in Doucette's cup of hot *chocolat* it had been downhill all the way.

At the time, the early morning walk along the beach, the combination of the sun, the sea and the sand had acted like a tonic. Pommes Frites had been in his element, dashing in and out of the water at every possible moment; taking pleasure out of presenting them with pieces of unwanted timber, sniffing rocks.

Having stumbled across a likely looking waterside café, they decided to take *petit dejeuner* then and there rather than wait until they were back at the hotel. At the time, as she sipped her freshly squeezed orange juice and helped herself from a basket of brioche still warm from the oven, Doucette happily agreed that Paradise might well be constructed along similar lines.

It was also a matter of accord that only in France would you find a humble beach café serving drinking *chocolat* made from granules supplied by Weiss of St. Etienne; almost on a par with Angelina's in the rue de Rivoli, back home in Paris; and *they* used a whole bar of chocolate in theirs.

It felt as though it had all been meant, and perhaps it had been.

Seconds later, the ball, propelled by an over-enthusiastic *Sapeur-Pompier*, one of a group playing nearby, sent the contents of the cup flying over her new beach dress, and the euphoric mood took a nose-dive.

All the signs suggested that recapturing it would be a slow and tedious, not to say expensive business, with no guarantee of success at the end of the day.

In retrospect, it had perhaps been a mistake to suggest that she shouldn't have ordered a *grande tasse de chocolat* in the first place, rather than a *demi*.

Thanking his lucky stars that the liquid had missed the Director's new lap-top by a matter of millimetres had been another error of judgement on his part, but it had been an instinctive reaction.

All that being so, he could hardly blame Doucette for obeying her own instincts. Grabbing hold of the ball, she thrust it into her beach bag, pulled the draw-string tight, and refused to let go.

Consternation reigned, but she wouldn't budge, and it was pursed lips all round as names and addresses were exchanged. Pommes Frites looked disappointed too, for he had been hoping to join in the game.

Mortified beyond measure, Monsieur Pamplemousse followed his wife back to the hotel, this time taking a path at the top of the beach, which was quicker than trudging through the dry sand.

In vain did he point out that the *Sapeurs-Pompiers* hadn't been playing football on the beach for fun. French firemen were members of a para-military organisation and such activities were part of their daily routine. It had to do with rigid discipline and the need to maintain a high standard fitness in order to cope with anything and everything that came their way.

Bombarding her with statistics on the exploits of their Paris colleagues while he tried to catch up with her: 200,000 calls a year, of which a mere 6,000 had to do with fires; the rest involving the rescue of attempted suicides from the Seine, removing wasps nests, dealing with drunken husbands and wife-beaters, drug addicts (who called on them because, unlike the police, they took no names), people trapped in lifts, leaking taps, rape, blocked drains. They had even been involved in the recent unsuccessful attempt to reanimate Francis le Belge, one of the last of the Marseilles Mafia

Godfathers, who had been gunned down in a Paris betting shop. Admittedly they hadn't known who they were dealing with at the time, but at least it demonstrated that their services were open to all, without fear or favour and regardless of his or her place in society.

He might just as well have saved his breath. It all went down like the proverbially lead balloon.

'If they're so versatile,' said Doucette crossly, 'perhaps they can do something about removing the stains from my dress.'

Sensing his master was fighting a losing battle, Pommes Frites tactfully disappeared, leaving them to their own devices.

On the way they engaged in a fruitless search for a boutique which included in its daily schedule the faintest possibility of being open before ten o'clock in the morning, and having found a maid already hard at work in their room, Monsieur Pamplemousse established two things.

First, he not only had to prepare a report on the *Au Soleil d'Or*, but also there were various pieces of new equipment the Director had landed him with, and if he didn't get down to it soon he never would.

Secondly, rather than trek into Nice with him, Doucette was perfectly happy to spend the morning by herself on the hotel's private beach.

'Wearing nothing but my bathing costume?' had been her response to his invitation.

She gazed at her flowered reflection in the long mirror attached to the inside door of the 1920's wardrobe. 'I suppose I shall have to make do with this old wrap. It's years since I last wore it. You don't think it is too short?'

'It is exactly right, Couscous,' said Monsieur Pamplemousse.

Doucette looked at him suspiciously. 'You always say that.'

He stifled a sigh. Some days you couldn't win. Gathering up his belongings, he beat a hasty retreat.

Back at the café he placed a repeat order for *petit dejeuner* and settled himself down to work. To his relief, the *Sapeurs-Pompiers* were nowhere to be seen, and apart from an occasional drone from a passing boat, all was at peace with the world.

Opening the lid of the computer, he reached for a fresh *croissant*, closed his eyes, and began marshalling his thoughts before starting work.

He had woken early, not so much through the strange surroundings – he was used to that, but because the events of the previous evening were still fresh in his mind. The Capricorn in him disliked having to admit defeat, even over such a comparatively minor problem as taking delivery of the Director's picture, which was, after all, one of the prime reasons for their visit.

Doucette had no such problems. When he'd pressed the button to raise the electrically operated shutters and sunlight flooded the room, she simply gave a grunt and turned over. There was no need for him to move around on tip-toe, but he had done so as a matter of course.

Hearing the clink of china, he'd looked down from the balcony and found he wasn't the only one awake by a long way. Several couples were already having breakfast on the terrace. Sparrows, clearly old hands at the game, gathered in an expectant row along the balustrade waiting for crumbs, and on a concrete area by the water's edge tables were already being made ready for lunch.

Pommes Frites was also out and about, acting in a supervisory capacity, chasing after a nut-brown beach attendant as he hurried past, bow-legged beneath a pile of blue and white striped mattresses.

The sommelier appeared, carrying a tray-load of glasses. Out of uniform and with her hair down, he hardly recognised her. She looked like a schoolgirl.

A speedboat, negotiating a line of yellow marker buoys, headed towards the pier, executed a sharp turn at the last possible moment and brought an early morning skier safely to rest at exactly the right spot as the driver cut his engine. The girl removed her skis, gave a thank-you wave, then climbing the steps and began sluicing herself down under a fresh water shower.

There was no sign of the fishing boat that had tied up the night before.

On the other side of the bay a match-stick figure rose into the air beneath a parachute, hovered for a moment or two, then pancaked into the sea.

It was the best part of the day; the hour or two before the crowds began to arrive.

He fell to thinking about his report. Recipient of two Stock Pots in Le Guide and an equal number of rosettes in Michelin, the hotel also enjoyed an entry in Relais et Chateaux, where it was described as being like a precious jewel set in a ribbon of gold; a statement it would be hard to argue with. In many ways it was a relic of by-gone age; to the days before property developers moved in, gobbling up every available piece of land that could conceivably be built on.

But then the *Côte d'Azur* was like that. Just as there were times when you felt it was hell on earth and must one day sink beneath the weight of all the concrete development, you turned a corner and found somewhere like *Au Soleil d'Or*; to all intents and purposes on another planet.

As for *dîner*. That had been hard to fault. The *pistou* with which they had begun the meal was a reminder that the great joy of being in Provence was the quality of the produce, and one the main reasons why the hôtel's restaurant enjoyed two Stockpots in Le Guide.

For the main course they had chosen c*anette laquée au miel de lavande* – fillets of duck breast brushed with lavender honey, simmered in a vegetable and herb stock, then browned, caramelized, and served with braised tomatoes and red peppers. The accompanying salad, the freshly picked raspberries that followed, had all been beyond reproach. With it they had drunk local wines; a *Côtes de Provence* white, and a robust Domain Tempier red from Bandol, served chilled. Both complemented the food in a way which greater wines would have been hard put to match.

It was high time he recaptured the essence of it all on paper. With over 500 questions on the standard report form to be answered, he needed to make a start while everything was still fresh in his mind. But before that, he had other matters to report on.

Creeping back into the bedroom, he went to Le Guide's travelling case and carefully removed the first of the Director's latest toys – a sub-miniature lap-top. Half the depth of a normal one, it even had a tiny video camera built into the lid.

Returning to the balcony he placed the computer and its accompanying accessories on the table, opened the lid and having pressed the start button, began to read through the instructions.

In the early days, when Le Guide's founder had first introduced the case, it had been a modest affair, containing just a few basic items. An austere man, and with only Paris and its environs to cover on his Michaux *bicyclette*, Monsieur Hippolyte Duval had deemed a few tins of emergency rations, a bottle of iodine, some bandages and a note-pad more than sufficient for his needs. In the fullness of time, with the arrival of the pneumatic tyre, a puncture repair outfit had been added, but for many years there matters had rested.

It was only after he retired and handed over the reins to Monsieur Leclercq that things began to change. What had started out as a simple cardboard attaché case small enough to slip into a wickerwork basket attached to the handlebars of his bicycle, grew into a sizeable piece of luggage made of thick leather. And as it grew in size, so it grew in complexity and weight.

A recent article in L'Escargot, Le Guide's staff magazine, had raised the subject. An unattributed pen and ink drawing (although everyone knew it was the work of the editor – Calvet) showed an Inspector toiling up a mountain pass followed by two Sherpas carrying the case between them. Rubbing salt into the wound, an anonymous writer in the letters column had suggested adding a wheel to all four corners.

As ever, Monsieur Leclercq had risen to the bait; and gone over the top. Miniaturisation was now a key element in his thinking, and science hadn't let him down: indeed, science showed it had every intention of keeping one step ahead for many years to come.

The new lap-top was a good example. Although he wouldn't have admitted it to Doucette, Monsieur Pamplemousse couldn't wait to try it out.

The set-up complete, he used the tracking button in the centre of the keyboard to manoeuvre the arrow over the Smart Capture icon and pressed the Enter key.

A second or so later the image on the screen reminded him forcibly that he had yet to shave. He could practically count the whiskers on his chin.

Having transferred the image onto the computer's memory, he tried rotating the tiny lozenge-size camera through 180 degrees so that its lens was facing out to sea. A large motor vessel swam into view, heading towards a landing stage further along the coast. The maroon and blue stars and oblong blocks of a Panamanian flag of convenience were crystal clear against the background of the sky.

He felt tempted to call his wife before recording it, then changed his mind. Doucette valued her beauty sleep and she wouldn't thank him.

The tip of his index finger having grown numb through using the tiny button, Monsieur Pamplemousse turned his attention to another of the Director's purchases; a miniature hand-held dictating machine – half the size of the new mobile phone – but with voice-recognition facilities.

Connecting it to the lap-top, he added a CD player

attachment, inserted a disc and reached for the instruction manual. At least its five different languages were separated; the very worst scenario was having five different languages for each paragraph. Once again though, as with the lap-top, he couldn't help wondering why Monsieur Leclercq had chosen to purchase the English model. Perhaps it was simply that both being new on the market, a French version wasn't yet available. Being a leader of fashion had its disadvantages. All the same, it struck him that 'Please write to Mr Wright right now,' must be a bit of a tongue twister for an English person, let alone anyone unaccustomed to the language.

'What are you doing, Aristide?' Doucette appeared in her dressing gown. 'I thought I heard voices.'

'It is the very latest in voice-operated software, Couscous,' said Monsieur Pamplemousse proudly. 'In future, instead of typing in my report I shall be able to speak it. But first it has to become accustomed to my voice.'

'It would be nice if other people had the chance to get accustomed to it once in a while,' said Doucette pointedly.

She peered over his shoulder at the screen. 'Write... write... write... If that's the best it can do I hate to think what it will make of last night's meal – a lot of gobbledegook I shouldn't wonder. It isn't even in French.'

'Patience, Couscous,' said Monsieur Pamplemousse. 'One out of three isn't bad for a start.'

'You need the man who was at the next table,' mused Ducette. 'His English was almost as good as his French. It could have been that he is from the Loire, of course...'

Monsieur Pamplemousse pretended he hadn't heard. He was rapidly taking a dislike to the other guest, whoever he was.

'Anyway, I thought you said it was a matter of saving space.' Doucette gazed at the tangle of wires spread out across the table. 'If you ask me it's worse than ever.'

'Even at this very moment, Couscous,' said Monsieur Pamplemousse, enunciating his words carefully for the benefit of the lap-top, whilst at the same time turning the screen away from his wife in case it made heavy weather of the endearment, 'scientists all over the world are doubtless working on the problem. By this time next year they will have come up with the answers. All the optional extras will be part and parcel of the whole. You mark my words. We are on the threshold of a paperless society. Best of all, this lap-top slips into my trouser leg pocket and takes up no more room than the notepad.'

'Things may be getting smaller,' said Doucette, 'but your fingers certainly aren't. Anyway, by this time next year they will probably have invented something that makes it all redundant. As for a paperless society, I shall believe it when I see it. A small packet of paper used to last you months. Now you buy it 500 sheets at a time. People no longer write letters, but they use more paper than ever, what with their faxes and their emails.'

Monsieur Pamplemousse sighed. Some people were left entirely unmoved by the manifold wonders of science. 'How about a walk before breakfast?' he suggested.

'I thought you would never ask...' Doucette's voice took on a dream-like quality and faded away as she padded off in the direction of the bathroom.

Left on his own, Monsieur Pamplemousse reached out to shut the lid of his computer only to discover... horror of horrors... It had seized up! No matter how hard he wrestled with it, it simply refused to budge.

'*Sacré bleu! Nom d'un nom!*' He could hardly believe it.

'*Merde!*' Banging on the table out of sheer frustration he woke with a start to find his fist covered in grease and the sound of a baby crying.

A squashed packet lay in front of him, a sodden mess of gold foil and butter. The bawling child and its owners – an English couple by the look of it, lobster red – were sitting at a nearby table. They stared at him uneasily, the mother making cooing noises as she tried to soothe her offspring. As soon as they saw Monsieur Pamplemousse glaring at them they looked the other way as though nothing had happened.

Wiping the stains from his Cupillard Rième wristwatch he saw it registered a few minutes short of 9.30. He must have been asleep for over half an hour.

Recovering himself as best he could, Monsieur Pamplemousse blew some *croissant* crumbs from the lap-top's keyboard and pressed the power switch.

While the machine was booting itself up, spewing out facts and figures at a speed too fast to read, he caught sight of the Russian he'd mentally christened Nikita. He was seated at a table at the far end of the small terrace in deep discussion with another man who had his back to the café. The second man had close-cropped grey hair. Expensively dressed in a mid-blue silk suit, each time he made a gesture with his right hand there was a sparkle from a gold bracelet.

Acting on an impulse, Monsieur Pamplemousse set up the mini-camera facility, rotating the pod until both men filled the frame.

Choosing his moment, he gave a friendly wave. It wasn't reciprocated, but the Russian said something to the second man, who glanced round briefly.

Monsieur Pamplemousse captured the moment and stored it for reference in the computer's memory. It was a very satisfactory experiment in covert information gathering. With no tell-tale click of a shutter, he could see all sorts of possible uses for it. He was also impressed at the speed at which the automatic exposure had corrected itself in order to compensate for the second man's swarthy appearance, somewhere midway between the blue of the suit and his white shirt.

Getting down to work at long last, he began typing out a preliminary heading for his report on how the new equipment was functioning.

Despite Doucette's earlier comments, his fingers ran smoothly over the keyboard.

Except . . . for a moment or two he sat nonplussed, staring

at the words on the screen: *Qnylyse Fonctionelle Eauip;ent Nouvelle q Qristide Pq,ple,ousse;;;*

Slowly the truth dawned on him. Monsieur Leclercq had been sold a pup – or rather two pups. Not only was the voice-activated programme for the dictating machine an English version, but so, too, was the lap-top's keyboard! Hence the Anglo-Saxon QWERT arrangement of the alphabet.

It was not a good beginning. Ill omens were rife. He was glad Doucette wasn't with him.

Closing down the programme in disgust, he waited for the screen to go dark, then closed the lid. No doubt there would be ways of changing the language electronically. Doubtless he could choose to work in Afghanistan if the Director so wished, but that wasn't the point. It would still mean the tops of the keys would have to be swapped around in order to avoid confusion and he had better things to do with his time.

The sooner he collected the picture for Monsieur Leclercq, the sooner he would be able to relax and enjoy his holiday.

Glancing up, he saw the two men were no longer there. Presumably had they had slipped away while he wasn't looking.

Bidding the English couple a polite good morning in gobbledegook, he went on his way. It could have been Greek for all the reaction he got, although the woman did give him a sickly smile.

Back at the hotel he found two police cars parked outside, along with a British registered Rover and a top of the range black Mercedes-Benz S-Class with all-round tinted glass and an 06 Alpes Maritimes registration.

One of the uniformed policemen eyed him curiously, as though trying to place him. His time in the Paris Sûreté still followed him around. The affair at the Folies that had led to his early retirement seemed to be indelibly etched on people's memories. Short of growing a beard he would have to grin and bear being recognised wherever he went for a long time to come. There were times when he might just as well have had his face on a WANTED poster and have done with it.

Pommes Frites was nowhere to be seen. For some reason best known to himself he had been acting very independently since their arrival. Monsieur Pamplemousse put it down to the holiday spirit. No doubt he would turn up when it suited him, and with the driver of the hotel courtesy coach into Antibes looking as though he was about to leave, he made a snap decision and climbed aboard.

A little way along the road, just past the first bend, he noticed a huge silver American Airstream caravan trailer parked in a lay-by cut in the side of the hill. There was no sign of a towing vehicle and it had an air of semi-permanence about it.

In Antibes he was just in time to catch the 10.22 *Transports Express Régionaux* double-decker train to Nice. Choosing the top deck, he found himself in a carriage surrounded by American Mormons. Smartly-dressed and freshly scrubbed, wearing their metal name badges with obvious pride, they all looked too young to be called "Elders". The world was growing more cosmopolitan by the day. The last time he had taken a train on that line, admittedly some years ago, it had been full of genuinely elderly local ladies on their way to market.

Gare Nice St. Augustin came and went and with it the once thriving Victorine film studios. It was hard to visualise it having been the setting for *Les Enfants du Paradis*, the first film he and Doucette had ever seen together. Given the almost constant roar of jet aircraft taking off from the airport on the other side of the railway track it wouldn't be easy to make its equivalent nowadays.

Afterwards they had ended up eating *couscous* at a small North Africa restaurant near Place Clichy, and the name had remained a term of endearment ever since.

Five minutes later they arrived at the *Gare Nice-Ville*.

Picking up a street map from the Tourist Office on his way out, and seeing a long queue outside the ticket-kiosk on the far side of the square, he took another chance and jumped on a local Sunbus which was about to depart.

Handing the driver 3f 50 in exchange for a plastic card marked 1 *voyage solo*, he validated it in the machine and sat back to take in his surroundings as they headed down the wide main street towards the sea.

So far, so good. Already he felt in a better mood. With luck he would be back at the hotel in time for lunch on the beach.

At the bottom of the avenue Jean Medicin they entered the vast Place Masséna with its Italian-style arcaded buildings, their facades stuccoed in red ochre, the pavements crowded with shoppers and window-gazing tourists. Taking a left, the bus headed inland again alongside the landscaped area acting as a roof to the Paillon river. Now relegated to being a mere underground stream, it had for centuries been the dividing line between the old city of Nice and the new.

It still had its moments of fame, of course. In 1976 it had been the setting for one of the great bank robberies of all time. *Un "Coup" Monumental* Nice-Matin had called it. In total the haul had been the equivalent of over $14,00,000,000.

Monsieur Jacques Genet, the *directeur* at the time, must still suffer nightmares thinking about it.

A little away along the boulevard Jean Jaures he saw what he was looking for: the restaurant L'Univers – Christian Plumail. It was time to get off.

Bernard still waxed lyrical about an *entrée* he had there on the last inspection two years ago. An unlikely, but apparently wholly delicious *grande assiette* of tomatoes: stuffed, dried, roasted and plainly sliced, topped by a deliciously fresh tomato sorbet.

Bernard's confession at the annual staff get-together that he hadn't realised until then how many things one could do with a tomato had given rise to much ribald comment.

Entering the old town, Monsieur Pamplemousse began

working his way through the maze of narrow, winding streets and tiny squares, making for the harbour area, where most of the antique shops were located.

The tall 17th and 18th century Genoese seaside Baroque buildings lining the alleyways on either side, their wrought iron balconies festooned with flowers and washing hanging out to dry, stood as a permanent reminder that they had once belonged to Italy.

He felt like a *flâneur* of old, taking his morning stroll. From being poor and run down, there was now an embarrassment of riches. At ground level, nouveau art galleries and designer-dress shops were sandwiched between old-fashioned *bricolages* and bars, *charcuteries* and *fromageries*; food shops of all descriptions, whose owners were probably steadfastly refusing to sell out. It was very different to the first time he'd visited Nice, long before he had ever dreamed that one day he might become a food Inspector. In those days it had been almost a no-go area after dark.

It was hard to say who would win in the end, but there was hardly room for both.

Emerging into blinding sunshine he found himself outside the church of St-Martin-St-Augustin. Set into a wall directly opposite was a massive plaque dedicated to the memory of Catherine Ségurane, a local washerwoman who in 1543 achieved fame by mounting the ramparts and lowering her culottes in the face of a horde of invading Turks under the command of the infamous Admiral Barbarossa. Gazing up at her formidable *derrière* as she stooped to pick up her paddle, they had run for their lives. He didn't blame them.

Making his way down to the street which also bore her name, he stopped once again and took out a piece of paper the Director had given him in order to double-check it against his map. Although he hadn't registered it at the time, there was no name and no phone number, just the minimal address scribbled on a piece of lined paper torn from a notepad.

He didn't even recognise the handwriting. It certainly wasn't the Director's.

A line of schoolchildren snaking their way past nudged each other. One, braver than the rest, placed a sticky finger over the autoroute to Cannes as he went past.

'*Vous êtes ici, Monsieur,*' he called, and they hurried on their way laughing happily.

Monsieur Pamplemousse wondered what would have happened to the boy had he tried it on with Madame Ségurene. Probably another bottom would have been bared that morning, and it wouldn't have been hers.

He found the address he was looking for, sandwiched between a garage and a builder's yard at the end of an alleyway not far from the antique market in the "Village Ségurene". But this time his luck ran out. A roll-top shutter was in place over the front. The lock securing it looked new. On the other hand, if the other establishments in the immediate neighbourhood were anything to go by, most of them, including the garage, must do their business later in the day.

He tried banging on the shutter but there was no reply. While he was debating what to do next, a black Mercedes drew up at the end of the alleyway and a man got out. Dressed in plain clothes, he nevertheless reeked *Police Judiciaire*. There was something vaguely familiar about him, and his feigned surprise at seeing Monsieur Pamplemousse wouldn't have won him any prizes at the Comédie-Francaise.

Greetings exchanged, a gentle probe began. 'What brings you to this part of the world? Don't tell me you are in the antiques business now.'

Monsieur Pamplemousse was non-committal. 'I am looking into a certain matter for someone.'

The response was equally cryptic. 'Once a *flic* – always a *flic*, eh?'

'*Alors!*' Monsieur Pamplemousse gave a shrug. 'So the saying goes.' Having no wish to prolong the conversation, he glanced pointedly at his watch, then held out his hand. He received a firm shake in return.

'*Au revoir*. Take care how you go.' There was no offer of a lift.

As he made his way slowly down towards the harbour Monsieur Pamplemousse puzzled over the last remark. It could simply have been a question of territories, but it had also sounded remarkably like a serious warning. Or a straightforward threat! He wondered, too, about the Mercedes with its conspicuously anonymous dark glass windows behind which he had seen the outline of the man already making a phone call as the car moved away.

Leaving the main port with its array of luxury yachts behind, he crossed over the rue de Foresta and stopped for a moment or two in a little park overlooking the commercial harbour. A cargo boat with an Amsterdam registration was being loaded. It looked huge to his eyes. 5,000 tonnes? 10,000? He had no idea. Truffert, another of his colleagues, would have known. He had spent most of his life at sea before joining Le Guide.

Whatever the tonnage was now, it would be considerably more by the time it set sail. As far as the eye could see the quay was lined with huge white bags of cement and more were arriving by the minute. Each one must weigh a tonne or more. The ship was riding high out of the water and each time its crane reached over the side to hoist another load on board – ten bags at a time - there was a distinct roll.

It was like watching a ballet, and as so often happened when thoughts ran free he found himself back at the antique shop.

Why would anyone want to put him off? And had the officer arrived by chance? It was almost as though he'd been waiting round the corner expecting someone to turn up.

At the far end of the quay a ferry arrived from Corsica and almost immediately began to disgorge its load; cars and vans rather than cabin trunks. Air transport had taken away a lot

44

of the romance of travel, and with it the excitement of arriving in a strange port at a leisurely pace. Nowadays the shock of encountering a strange culture often had to be absorbed in a matter of seconds.

A small boy on roller blades buzzing to and fro behind him interrupted his train of thought and, it being a day for spur of the moment decisions, rather than follow the noisy traffic-ridden boulevard Princesse de Monaco round the peninsula, he set off up the hill leading to the Colline du Château, the huge mound overlooking the harbour on one side and the Baie des Anges on the other.

It was where the Greeks had built their acropolis, only to have it demolished by the Savoyards, who replaced it with a citadel. That, too, had suffered a similar fate at the hands of the Sun King, Louis XIV.

Halfway up the hill he entered the Christian cemetery and stopped to get his breath back. A woman in black armed with a bucket of water and a scrubbing brush went past, joining the rest of her family on what was clearly a regular cleaning operation. An attendant waved a warning finger at a small group of Japanese tourists posing nearby, directing them to a notice on the gate saying the taking of photographs was forbidden.

Making his way to the outer wall, he looked out across the valley and was once again reminded of the bank robbery. Between where he was standing and the surrounding hills, the huge Palais des Expositions stood astride the entrance to the underground river where it had all started. A bare trickle now, but at certain times of the year, when the snows melted, it was probably a different matter.

Led by one Albert Spaggiari, who had managed to acquire a plan showing the lay-out of the sewer system, the thieves made their way down the Paillon, located the foundations of the main branch of the Société Générale Bank at 8 Avenue Jean Médecin, then tunnelled their way into the vaults. Once inside, they welded the giant twenty-ton Fichet-Bauche door to its frame and spent the whole of one weekend quietly going through the strong boxes, the contents of which many owners had no wish to reveal.

Where there is great wealth, crime is never far away, and Nice was certainly no exception. He was glad he hadn't had to work on the case. By all accounts there had been too much pulling of strings behind the scenes for his liking; too many nameless high-ups who'd had good reason to soft pedal the whole affair.

By contrast, the adjoining Jewish cemetery further up the hill was a sad affair; full of reminders of families torn apart by the Holocaust. It began just inside the entrance where there were two urns; one containing ashes from the victims of concentration camps and the other rendered down grease for making soap.

The sole occupant, a small man in a dark lounge suit several sizes too big for him, disappeared behind a tomb as soon as he entered, almost as though still fleeing for his life. Monsieur Pamplemousse left him to it.

Passing a cascade further down the hill a few minutes later, he automatically looked round for Pommes Frites. He would have revelled in its ice-cold water.

There was a moment when he thought he was being followed, but then decided he was imagining things – it was only a mother and child in a push-chair. All three of them jumped at the sound of an explosion nearby and the child started to cry.

'*C'est normale.*' The woman gave the child a pat. 'It is the noonday cannon,' she added for Monsieur Pamplemousse's benefit. 'Or rather, it is the explosive device that has replaced it. It is not so nice.'

'Nothing is for ever,' said Monsieur Pamplemousse.

He remembered now. The firing of a canon had been instituted by an Englishman who liked to make sure his meals arrived on time no matter where he happened to be. Such an admirable device was not to be ignored. Following the signs to the *ascenseur* he quickened his pace and was just in time to catch one going down.

Doucette was right, of course. They had no idea what size the Monsieur Leclercq's "work of art" would be. The Director had been characteristically vague on that score. He couldn't think why he hadn't asked at the time, but then neither had she.

Paying his Fr.3.80 to the Madame at the bottom he registered the fact that *chiens* were half price. Given that Pommes Frites took up enough room for two adults it would be good value if he happened to join him on a return visit; especially if they did what he should have done in the first place – used it to go up rather than down.

Entering the Cours Saleya through the first of the old arched gateways memories came flooding back. Teeming with life and colour; it was no wonder that when Matisse lived there his doctor tried to persuade him to wear dark glasses to protect his vision.

Beyond the dazzling display of flowers – peonies, roses, carnations and lilies, lay the fruit and vegetable market with its mouth-watering displays of freshly picked apples, apricots, cherries and nectarines. Pyramids of pears and peaches fought for space alongside huge red tomatoes and tiny ripe Ogen melons from Cavaillon. Aubergines and peppers gave way to mounds of green and black olives and great fat bunches of garlic. There were tables laid out with *glacé* fruits, others with bowls of multicoloured dried herbs; saffron, cayenne and spices of all descriptions.

Around the perimeter of the market small cafés had local specialities on display: *pan bagna* – bread rolls split in half, sprinkled with olive oil and filled with tomatoes, green peppers and black olives; *pissaladièra* – pastry shells containing anchovy paste, olives and onion purée. Copper pans stood ready for the old favourite, *socca*. Made with olive oil and chick-pea flour, they had to be eaten piping hot.

Through a gap in the crowd he suddenly caught sight of

the man from the Jewish cemetery. Only a few stalls away, he was holding an artichoke up to the light with his left hand, as though studying it. With his other hand he held a mobile phone to his ear.

As their eyes met Monsieur Pamplemousse found himself wondering how many others in the world were doing exactly the same thing at that very moment, and decided that statistically not many, if any at all. Could there be a woman somewhere, drumming impatiently because he was late home with the shopping? Somehow doubting it, he hurried on his way.

Passing the Opera House, he noticed the door to the Église St-François-de-Paule on the opposite side of the road was open. Taking advantage of a stationary delivery van caught up in the traffic, he skirted round the back of it, ignored the outstretched hand of a beggar hovering on the pavement, and slipped inside.

He was beginning to wish he'd brought Pommes Frites with him after all. Pommes Frites would have seen him off whoever he was.

Brief encounters

After the noise and bustle of the Cours Saleya the atmosphere inside the church was an all-enveloping oasis of calm and serenity. Its richly baroque décor made it feel as though he had entered a different world.

An earnest group of tourists gathered round a carved olive wood statue to his left, comparing an entry in their guidebook to the real thing, eyed him curiously as he looked around for somewhere to hide.

The theatrical arrangement of stage boxes on either side of the altar was tempting, but grilles barred the way and he had no idea how to reach them from behind.

Crossing himself, he wondered whether to join the few silent worshippers dotted around on either side of the centre aisle, then decided against it. They were nearly all elderly women. He would stand out like a sore thumb. Turning his back on them, he hesitated for a moment before gently opening an exit door to his left. As he had hoped, it led into what was virtually a tiny room, the left side of which was made up of a second glass-panelled door affording a discrete view of the street.

He was just in time to see the man appear from behind the van, clearly following the same route. The artichoke had been discarded, but he was still talking into the mobile; his eyes darting everywhere before he turned and began retracing his steps.

Monsieur Pamplemousse slipped out of the church while he had the chance. Feeling in his pocket for a coin, he placed it in the beggar's hand in exchange for muttered directions, then continued on his way as fast as he could without actually drawing attention to himself.

Crossing the vast Albert 1st gardens straddling the one-time estuary to the Paillon, he followed a winding path threading its way in and out of the palm trees. Keeping a bandstand to his left as instructed, and doing his best to avoid the occasional sudden flick from a watering system which threatened to soak any passers-by who weren't careful, he set about negotiating the Avenue du Verdun on the far side. Pursued by a hail of impatient horn-blowing, he headed towards the rue de Masséna, looking for the second of Bernard's recommended restaurants: the Villa d'Este.

It was yet another area of Nice that had changed since his last visit. Apart from an occasional service vehicle nosing its way through the crowd, the street was closed to normal traffic. Tables and chairs from restaurants nestled cheek by jowl with designer boutiques. They spilled out on either side, taking up every available space. He glanced at his watch. Although it was barely a quarter to one, most were already more than half full.

'Try the *Jambon de Parme veritable* with melon,' had been Bernard's advice. 'You won't get better this side of the Italian border – if then.'

Seating himself between two girls, each with a mobile phone, Monsieur Pamplemousse placed his order.

Watching the ham being cut, he immediately felt at home. The twisting, the caressing, the squeezing motion that went into the operation was both an act of love and a work of art. Alongside the carver, another man wielding a long wooden paddle was feeding pizzas into a wood-fired oven.

Taste buds began to salivate in anticipation.

Adding a *demi Bandol rosé* and a San Pellegrino to his order, he helped himself to some bread and sat back prepared to enjoy himself.

Not to be outdone in the electronic stakes, he removed the lap-top from his trouser pocket, powered it, and set up the Smart Capture facility. It hardly merited a passing glance from either of the girls.

Two roller bladers gliding effortlessly in and out of pedestrians on the crowded concourse, missing people by a few centimetres either way, swooped into close-up, their faces momentarily distorted, then disappeared again just as quickly. He let them go.

The ham, when it arrived, was exactly as Bernard had described it, *parfait*! So *parfait* in fact, he almost missed seeing the Putin look-alike hurry into view.

As soon as the man realised he'd been spotted he did a U-turn. Pausing outside another restaurant further along the street, he pretended to read the menu. Reaching for the keyboard, Monsieur Pamplemousse was just in time to record the image as he turned to go inside. He typed in the time – 12.55 – and filed the picture away under PUTIN.

He wondered how the man had caught up with him again so quickly. Ignoring the beggar outside the church the first time had been a mistake, but at least his tip on the way out ought to have made up for it.

Checking the loose change in his pocket, he realised that in his haste instead of giving the man ten francs to ensure his silence, he must have given him the 20 centimes coin he'd received in his change from the lift attendant.

It was a case of the *clochard*'s revenge and no mistake.

The girl to his right had ordered a pasta dish of some substance. Checking with the menu he identified it as the Niçoise version of *picagge verdi*, made without sausage, but with Swiss chard, spinach and a little finely chopped salt pork. She carried on her telephone conversation as she picked at it with a fork.

The girl on his left was already attacking a giant pizza. Piping hot from the oven, it was large enough for a whole family. She, too, carried on with her conversation.

Dressed in black trouser suits, with dark sun-glasses and matching black lacquered finger-nails, both girls looked cool in every sense of the word. Both were pencil slim, although from their conversation more 2H than 3B, and he didn't exactly envy their boyfriends.

Nearing the end of his ham, he finished off the wine, then

eyed their plates enviously. If they could get away with it, there was no reason why he shouldn't too. In the interests of research and of keeping his adversary kicking his heels, he felt tempted to give one or other a try. On the other hand...

It could have been sheer coincidence that the man was following the same path as he was. Stranger things happened all the time, but instinct told him it wasn't, and instinct was something you ignored at your peril. Shutting down the laptop, he stowed it away in his trouser pocket. There was only one way to find out. Waving his napkin he caught the waiter's eye.

'*Oui, Monsieur. Il conto.*' His bill was ready and waiting.

This time luck was with him. Choosing his moment, he made a quick exit while he was screened from view by a group of tourists studying the menu on a metal display stand.

The look on the man's face as he gave him a nod while strolling past was a study in frustration. Skirting round a large woman with a sun-hat and oversize Reeboks trying unsuccessfully to pay for an ice-cream cone with a dollar bill, he slipped into a boutique further along the rue Masséna. Putting a rack of clothes in the middle of the floor between himself and the door, he waited.

'*Monsieur?*' A girl emerged from behind a counter at the rear of the shop and looked at him enquiringly. '*Qu'est-ce que vous désirez?*'

'*Je regarde seulement,*' said Monsieur Pamplemousse hastily. 'I am only looking.'

The last thing he wanted was to be trapped inside the shop. Unless...he ran his eye along the rack...

Twenty minutes later, having made sure he wasn't being followed, armed with a carrier bag and a copy of *Le Figaro*, he boarded a single-decker Metrazur Ventimiglia-Cannes stopping train for Antibes. There were no Mormons on board as far as he could see; in fact it was less than a quarter full.

Feeling in need of a quiet think, he placed the carrier bag

on the opposite seat in the hope that it would save him being disturbed, settled down, then immediately wished he hadn't.

On the other side of the aisle two Englishmen were holding forth. It was marginally worse than the girls he'd had to endure at lunchtime. At least the latter had kept their voices down.

Burying his head in the *journal*, he tried hard not to listen in, but it wasn't easy.

'When I get to Gatwick I have to drive all the way to Haywards Heath against the flow of the traffic.'

'Hard luck!'

'The thing is, what am I going to do about the *langouste* in the boot of the car?'

Everyone had their problems. Some seemed more pressing than others.

There was no mention in the *journal* of the previous evening's affair at the hotel, but then it would have been surprising if there had been. It was hardly an event of national importance. He should have picked up the local *Nice Matin* for that.

Farmers were blockading the roads in Brittany. A group of them had emptied a trailer-load of manure on the steps of a town hall. Nurses were holding a protest march in Paris, demanding more pay and better working conditions. Nothing changed.

Removing the lap-top from his trouser leg pocket, Monsieur Pamplemousse opened the lid and pressed the start button. Conscious that the others went quiet as soon as they heard the burst of music accompanying the automatic booting up operation, he returned to his *journal* and waited.

The Euro had lost a couple of points against the dollar. Charles Aznavour was appearing at the Palais des Congrès in Paris.

Perversely, he now found himself straining to hear what was being said on the other side of the aisle.

'Extraordinary really. When you think the first hard disk on an IBM was like a flywheel. Weighed a ton.'

'Coated with the same paint they used on the Golden Gate Bridge, so they say.'

'Their latest microchip is 800 times thinner than a human hair.'

'How about the Intel Pentium 4? 10 million transistors and several kilometres of wiring packed into a square centimetre.'

'That's progress for you.'

'Did you see where he kept it?'

'Inside his trouser leg! Something new every day.'

'It'll never catch on.'

'Bet you he's got some kind of magic act. Kid's parties, perhaps. Or cabaret.'

'Ideal for a rep, of course.'

Monsieur Pamplemousse wondered for a moment what a rep was, then he remembered. It was the English term for a *voyageur de commerce*. Which, in a way, he supposed he was.

'Looks more like a doctor to me. Probably entering up his notes.'

'Or a policeman.'

'Watch it!' They dissolved into chuckles at the thought.

All the same, they had made it in four. Monsieur Pamplemousse scrolled back to the first picture. Did he really look like a policeman? He couldn't see it himself. But then, you never did see yourself as others saw you.

He felt tempted to pass some kind of comment. It didn't take an ex-detective to guess they must be heading for the International Science Park at Valbonne Sophia-Antopolis; the French equivalent of Silicon Valley in California.

It was hard to imagine why anyone would want to leave a *langouste* in the boot of their car – harder still to see what the problem might be if they did. Unless, of course, the man was flying back to England. In which case it probably smelled to high heaven by now. If he were travelling with hand baggage he wouldn't be too popular.

Glancing down at his lap-top he realised the screen-saver was on. Restoring the picture, he entered the Still Viewer. The journey provided a good opportunity to recap on the pictures he'd stored. At least he didn't have to wait for them to be processed.

There was a pause, then the last shot taken outside the restaurant came up on the screen. He'd been a fraction late on the button. The Putin look-alike was already half out of frame on the left-hand side, carefully avoiding his gaze as he went.

Shifting the pointer onto a sliding bar Monsieur Pamplemousse tried moving it along to the left, and found himself scrolling back at speed through the complete set of images he had captured during the day. Apart from the first mirror image of himself, he was building up a regular rogues' gallery.

The Englishmen had resumed their conversation, having changed the subject completely. He wondered if they always talked at the top of their voices, or whether it was because they assumed no one would understand what they were saying. Either way showed a kind of arrogance.

'Breast-feeding isn't allowed in our Houses of Parliament on the grounds that it's forbidden to bring refreshments into the Chamber.'

And they said the French were devious! He made a mental note to store it for future use. It would be a good conversation stopper.

The second picture of the boat with the Panamanian flag was followed by the one he'd taken at the beach café. He stared at the screen.

At the time he'd hardly registered the scene. Now, seeing it again as a static shot, it clicked home. The man turning his head briefly towards the camera was one and the same as the policeman he'd encountered in Nice. Admittedly he had been wearing sunglasses on the second occasion, but he recognised the jacket. It was food for thought.

He was half-right about the Englishmen. As the train approached Villeneuve-Loubet station the one with the problem awaiting him in his boot made ready to leave.

'Give my regards to the little woman. Have a good flight.'

'*Ciaou*! See you back at the ranch in a week's time.'

He gave a nod in Monsieur Pamplemousse's direction as he left. Monsieur Pamplemousse took pleasure in responding in English.

'Good luck with the *langouste*.'

It was like the proverbial water off a duck's back.

As the train gathered speed again, the vast curving terraces of the luxury apartments of the Marina-Baie des Anges came into view; a permanent eyesore to some, a way of life to others. It was followed by a long, straight stretch of parallel road and rail and a pebbled beach crowded with sun-worshippers.

He felt a momentary pang of remorse. His own "little woman" must have been looking forward to their unexpected time away together. His absence must be maddening for her, although over the years she had undoubtedly grown used to it. Much of their married life had been spent apart. Office hours as such hadn't existed during his time with the Paris *Sûreté*, and since working for Le Guide he spent more time away from home than ever. Pommes Frites saw more of him than she did, although even that didn't seem to be the case this time round. Not that he was happy lying on a beach all day, and luckily Doucette felt much the same way, although she was better at it than he was and enjoyed the opportunity for a swim.

That was another difference between them. Unless there was somebody near at hand, ready and willing to give him the kiss of life should something go wrong, he preferred being on dry land. Once out of his depth he quickly went into sinking mode.

As for the sun: prolonged exposure turned him lobster red rather than mahogany brown, leaving him feeling conspicuous amongst all the seasoned sun-worshippers. His preferred method of seeing it was from behind glass, preferably tinted when he was out driving, although that luxury was not on the list of optional extras for his *deux chevaux*.

Seeing Marineland flash past on his right, he began packing up his belongings.

Why did having tinted glass immediately make the occupants of a car objects of suspicion? In a sunny region like the Côte d'Azur it was a very sensible optional extra. He wondered if the Mercedes in Nice had been the same one that had been parked outside the hotel. On neither occasion had he taken a note of the number; something he would have done automatically in the old days.

But then one Mercedes looked very like another. Half the taxis in the area were Mercs. The one that had taken them to the hotel on their arrival had been an E Class. The diver had eyed Pommes Frites less than enthusiastically when he took advantage of the open door and climbed in the front seat, although he hadn't argued the point.

Unless things had changed very much since his day it was very unusual to find the police using one. In general, unless it was a covert operation, they operated a see and be seen policy. And even if it were a covert operation it was highly unsuitable. They would be more likely to use a battered old van. There was nothing more calculated to draw people's attention than having darkened windows. Passers-by immediately wanted to see inside, and if they couldn't they suspected the worst.

Bidding the remaining Englishman goodbye, he made his way to the rear of the carriage.

He was back rather sooner than he had expected. Although he hadn't achieved what he had set out to do, the journey hadn't been entirely wasted. Interesting; enjoyable; at times instructive.

Being without a car had been an unexpected bonus. Normally he felt lost without it. But he'd felt a curious sense of freedom wandering around. On the other hand, he'd missed having Pommes Frites for company. And he was no further ahead with tracking down the Director's painting. It was beginning to irk him, but *comme ci, comme ça*, you won some, you lost some.

The taxi rank outside Antibes station was empty, and a small queue had already formed. Wondering whether to take a stroll round the harbour, he looked at his watch.

There was time to spare before the hotel courtesy bus was due at the pick-up point.

Hearing the sound of a fairground going full blast from the direction of the port, he decided against it, opting instead to walk into the town.

Having got as far as the Place General de Gaulle, he was wondering whether to venture any further or call it a day, when he heard his name being called.

'Aristide!'

Turning, he saw an immaculate white-suited figure, a black object over one arm, and an English *journal* tucked under the other, emerging from a *librairie*.

'Monsieur Pickering! What are you doing here?'

'Staying at the same hotel, as a matter of fact. It's a small world. I saw you there last night – with Madame Pamplemousse, I imagine – not to mention the redoubtable Pommes Frites. But we didn't want to interrupt while you were all eating. Then, suddenly, there you were – gone.' He waved the *journal*. 'Can't do without the crossword. English papers don't arrive until the afternoon.'

'But this is wonderful!' Monsieur Pamplemousse felt a pang of guilt for having harboured uncharitable thoughts about the mysterious man at the next table. He saw Mr. Pickering only rarely. They communicated mostly by telephone, but over the years their friendship had blossomed. The last time they had met was when they were both involved with the ill-fated plan to launch a luxury airship service between their two countries. Monsieur Pamplemousse had been acting on Le Guide's behalf over the catering arrangements for the inaugural flight, and Mr. Pickering, revealing his connections with British Intelligence, had been on the trail of a terrorist. Their paths had become inextricably linked.

'Thought you'd given up this sort of thing,' said Mr. Pickering, 'but I suppose once a policeman, always a policeman.'

Monsieur Pamplemousse stared at him. It was the second time that day the phrase had been used.

'I am mostly here on holiday,' he said.

'Aah,' said Mr. Pickering cryptically. 'That's what my friend, Todd, says! You must meet him. Talking of which, if we don't hurry we shall miss the courtesy bus.'

As Monsieur Pamplemousse fell into step, Mr. Pickering gave him a sideways glance. 'Are you all right? You weren't limping the last time I saw you.'

'It is my lap-top,' said Monsieur Pamplemousse simply, pointing to his right leg.

'Ask a silly question,' said Mr. Pickering. He looked as though he was about to say more, but broke off in a flurry of introductions when they reached the pick-up point.

Monsieur Pamplemousse recognised the newcomer from Doucette's description.

Short, dark, thickset; the comparison with Tino Valentino was irresistible. Take away the baseball hat and the t-shirt depicting a road map of France he was wearing outside his denim trousers, swap them for a straw boater and a broad-striped blazer, and the picture would be complete. All the same, he couldn't quite visualise him singing Italian love songs to the accompaniment of a portable stereo.

'Is your wife also staying at the hotel?' he asked politely.

Todd shook his head.

'Todd is a DINK,' said Mr. Pickering.

'Double Income – No Kids', said Todd briefly. 'It's a kinda

cross between a mid-lifer and an empty-nester, plus the optional extras.'

Monsieur Pamplemousse found himself wondering where the extras came from.

'Being a master of disguise,' explained Mr. Pickering, 'to the likes of you and me Todd is in the Import-Export business, but to the outside world he runs a CIA Awareness Post. Or is it the other way round? I can never remember.'

Todd ignored the remark. 'I'll tell you what I am. I'm a Sentinel Chicken. That's one step away from being a third-ager retiree. Right?'

Seeing Monsieur Pamplemousse's puzzled expression as they boarded the bus, he waited until they were seated away from the others before elaborating.

'Back home they have chickens stationed in various strategic points, mostly Florida and California. They're on what's called mosquito surveillance duty. Every few weeks during the summer months they get tested for viral activity. Like in 1990 chickens in Florida detected encephalitis before it had a chance to spread. Usually they're in flocks of ten. Me, I'm a loner and I got myself no plans for going dual.

'You gotten any theories about what happened last night?'

'Last night?' Monsieur Pamplemousse did his best to keep up. *'Qu'est-ce que c'est passé?'*

'Todd means the body in the water,' explained Mr. Pickering. 'The one they deposited on the landing stage while we were having dinner.' He hesitated. 'Of course, I forgot. You had already gone up to your room by then.'

Monsieur Pamplemousse paused. 'I heard a commotion, but I hadn't realised they were dealing with a body. Perhaps it was someone from the hotel who had been for a late night swim and misjudged the currents. They can be very deceptive.'

'I think we can discount that possibility,' said Mr. Pickering.

'The guy was in a non-viable swimming condition,' broke in Todd.

'I thought Pommes Frites provided a very good summing-up of the situation,' continued Mr. Pickering. 'In his usual succinct way, with one brief howl he captured it quite beautifully: very Hound of the Baskervilles. For a moment or two it quite put me off my rhum baba.'

'Non-viable?' Monsieur Pamplemousse looked puzzled.

'Our transatlantic friends hate using the word "dead",' said Mr. Pickering. 'It is one of their more endearing qualities. He'd suffered a misadventure of high magnitude which led to a systems failure. Tell him how it came about, Todd.'

'He'd been surgically disarticulated. Know what I mean?'

Mr. Pickering savoured the phrase. 'Don't you love it?'

Monsieur Pamplemousse couldn't help but feel that the answer depended very much which side you happened to be on, but he kept his counsel, wondering instead how such an outwardly civilised person as Mr. Pickering could possibly harbour such thoughts.

On reflection, he supposed it went with the one accoutrement that seemed to accompany him wherever he went. Like his pipe, he was never without it. Monsieur Pamplemousse had long suspected it must conceal a weapon of some kind. A swordstick perhaps?

Why else would anyone, even the most urbane of Englishmen, be carrying a rolled umbrella on the Riviera in the middle of June?

The bus stopped short of the hotel to drop Todd off at the trailer caravan he'd seen earlier in the day. It didn't surprise him. Somehow the two went together.

'I'm glad you two have met,' said Mr. Pickering, as they waved goodbye. 'Todd's good to have around. Tough as old boots. Seen it all. First rate in an emergency. On your side.'

It sounded like the edited version of a CV. Monsieur Pamplemousse wondered what he had done to deserve it; or, perhaps more to the point, what might be expected of him at some future date.

The day that the rains came down

The day began with a fanfare from the bedside radio. It was followed by some pips and a dark brown voice, rich in Southern overtones. 'In the Alps,' it said, 'the carrot is golden and already cooked to perfection, but for the time being it is resting; hidden from view on a cushion of cauliflowers.'

'What *is* the man on about?' said Madame Pamplemousse sleepily. 'Anyone would think he was applying for a job with Le Guide. I thought he was supposed to be giving the weather forecast not reading from a menu.'

'It *is* the weather forecast.' Monsieur Pamplemousse emerged from the bathroom. 'He is simply saying that for the time being the sun is hidden behind some clouds. In total, rainfall on the Côte d'Azur is not so very much different to anywhere else in France. It just so happens that it generally comes all at once, so it is a case of making the most of it. Meteorologists latch on to any sign of a change and milk it for all it's worth. Think of having to say the same old thing day after day. They probably go to church Sundays and pray for a posting to Brittany where there is more weather than they would know what to do with.

'It is like being an airline pilot. After sitting in their seat for hours on end twiddling their thumbs while they are crossing the Atlantic, the moment of truth comes when they begin the final approach. A bumpy landing and they are cast in gloom for the rest of the day, a smooth one and they are walking on air.'

'If they were able to do that,' said Doucette, 'it would mean something had gone very wrong with their calculations.'

Monsieur Pamplemousse pretended he hadn't heard. 'If you ask me, he is hedging his bets.'

'Was, you mean,' said Doucette. 'I think he has finished. Now we shall never know.'

'Ssh! *Un moment.*' Monsieur Pamplemousse held a finger to his lips and was just in time to catch the sting in the tail. 'Beware! The signs are misleading. Remember the old saying: *Soleil rouge du matin fair trembler le marin?*' For the benefit of any Anglo-Saxon holiday-makers who happened to be listening the announcer lapsed into broken English: 'Red sky in ze morning – shephardy's warning.' 'What did I tell you?' said Monsieur Pamplemouse. 'Shephardy's warning!'

Operating the shutters, he unfastened the balcony door and felt a draft of warm air as it swung open. 'My grandmother used to say much the same thing whenever we had a long spell of hot weather: "It is too good to be true. Mark my words. We shall pay for it!".'

Outside the air did indeed feel heavy and overcast. The sky was covered by a mixture of grey and white cloud. Lacking any blue to reflect, the sea had an ominous, almost sullen look to it. So much for the inevitability of seeing the sunrise.

A solitary water-skier was making for harbour further along the coast. Nearer to the shore seagulls crowded together on the small pier, pecking furiously at anything they could find. The hotel was also hedging its bets. The man who was normally out early raking the sand was nowhere to be seen. Mattresses remained piled up alongside the parasols, while half the luncheon tables remained bare as staff gloomily awaited a decision from on high. Apart from the forecaster, bad weather was not a matter up for discussion on the Riviera; particularly where *hôtelièrs w*ere concerned.

'Aristide . . . come quickly . . .' At the sound of his wife's voice, Monsieur Pamplemousse rushed back into the room. It was a female news reader this time: '. . . the Nice Police are investigating the possibility that the dismembered body of a man found floating in the water off Cap d'Antibes on Tuesday evening may be the remains of a well-known Nice antique dealer who has been missing from his home since Tuesday. The cause of death has still to be established. We hope to have more details in our eleven o'clock bulletin.

'The Pope is continuing his tour of Basutoland with a visit to the cath...'

Madame Pamplemousse pressed the off button. 'How awful!' she exclaimed. 'That was the day we arrived. Aristide... you don't think...'

'If it is,' said Monsieur Pamplemousse, 'then Monsieur Leclercq's painting may well be at the bottom of the sea.' He was tempted to add 'or else hanging on someone's apartment wall,' but it felt too reminiscent of their previous evening's conversation for comfort.

'After we have had our *petit dejeuner* I think I may go along to the school,' he said instead.

'Must you, Aristide?' sighed Doucette, knowing the answer full well.

'It is just possible the man arrived early and arranged for the painting to be picked up.'

'And left no message? It hardly seems likely.'

'At least I shall have explored every avenue,' said Monsieur Pamplemousse. 'Our consciences will be clear.' Opening Le Guide's issue case, he removed the Leica R4 camera, dithered for a moment or two over the choice of film, and finally decided to load up with a spool of Ilford HP4. Storms on the stretch of coast south of the Alps were often dramatic. They lent themselves to black and white photography. Removing the standard 50 mm Summicron lens, he substituted the latest addition which was currently on test – a light-weight Tamron 28-300mm zoom, pocketed a couple of cloud filters and a spare film, then attached the motor-drive.

With luck he might get something spectacular for the front cover of the staff magazine. Calvet, the editor, was always on the look-out for something different and if the rumours were true that a more sophisticated version of it might be going on general sale, it could be an opportune moment.

Hearing the sound of voices and clinking china, he went out onto the balcony again.

The Russian family had arrived for breakfast: father, mother and a younger woman – he guessed she must be a nanny come interpreter since he had seen her translating the menu for them at dinner the previous evening.

The thickset man with the teeth who had also been present at the school play, and looked as though he might be a minder, was taking his seat at an adjoining table.

While he was watching, the child arrived. With her hair in pigtails and without make-up she looked almost human. She was wearing a school back-pack, and with her barrel-shaped torso she reminded Monsieur Pamplemousse of a Russian nesting doll, with its endless layers that come apart. He wondered what would be inside her. Would one ever get beyond the second layer? And once there, would it reveal a soft centre?

Acting on the spur of the moment, he powered the camera, switched to automatic, then crouched down so that he could use the top of the balcony as a rest while he zoomed in on the girl.

Almost as though they were linked by some kind of servo-mechanism, at the very moment when he pressed the shutter release she turned and stared straight up at him.

Hastily zooming out and panning away from her revealed the fact that for the second time in less than 48 hours, the whole group were now looking his way.

Monsieur Pamplemousse gave a tentative wave. It was met with icy stares all round; the child's eyes were the coldest of all. He felt almost tempted to look for a lens tissue to wipe away the frost.

What was the English saying about little girls being made of sugar and spice and all things nice? Either he'd got it wrong or she had a problem with her genes. He must check with Mr. Pickering.

'You are looking very furtive, Aristide. Is anything the matter?' Doucette joined him on the balcony as he was about to move. 'That man's ears look even worse in the daylight. I can see what is now. He's got no lobes.'

Ignoring the non-sequitor, Monsieur Pamplemousse converted his wave into an indication of the weather in general. 'It is not a day to spend on the beach, Couscous. What will you do while I am gone?'

'I half promised I would meet Madame Pickering,' said Doucette. 'Did you know she is a Judo black belt?'

'Is that why you are seeing her?' Leading the way back into the bedroom, he closed the door behind them.

'Of course not. It's just that it seems so unlikely.'

'It doesn't surprise me,' said Monsieur Pamplemousse. Nothing surprised him about the Pickerings. Mr. Pickering was one of those strange Englishmen with such diverse interests he was impossible to categorise. It was probably a case of like marrying like.

'Her name's Jan. It's short for Janet. And I guessed right – she's Scottish. She belongs to something called a Women's Institute – they make *confiture*. She has a gold medal for her roses. She goes clay pigeon shooting. *And* she bakes her own bread.'

'Perhaps she has a guilt complex,' said Monsieur Pamplemousse.

'I doubt it,' said Doucette. 'I think she is just one of those people who always has to be doing something. She also makes wine from oak leaves. Mr. Pickering says it's better than leaving them on the railway lines and holding up the trains. I'm not sure whether he was joking or not.'

'It is often hard to tell with *les Anglaises*,' said Monsieur Pamplemousse. 'Knowing his taste in wine I should have thought he would prefer them left where they had fallen.'

'Other people seem to lead such active lives,' persisted Doucette. 'Yesterday she was grumbling about being away. Apparently this week it is the local fête and she is usually in charge of the duck races. Do you think there is something wrong with me?'

'Of course not, *Couscous*.' Monsieur Pamplemousse gave his wife a hug. 'I'm sure you are just as busy in other ways.'

Madame Pamplemousse looked relieved. 'In that case you won't mind if I go into Antibes and visit the Picasso Museum with her.'

'Of course not.' Monsieur Pamplemousse tried not to sound too enthusiastic.

Last night at dinner Doucette and Madame Pickering had got on like a house on fire (he still found it hard to think of her as Jan) and it would solve the problem of going off on his own. His conscience would be clear.

The news item on the radio that morning was unsettling to say the least. He glanced at his watch. It was barely nine o'clock; too early to telephone Monsieur Leclercq. Anyway, what was there to say? That the man he was supposed to have met might have been "surgically disarticulated" as the American, Todd, would put it? There was no sense in worrying him unnecessarily.

'Do you think you should take a *parapluie*?' asked Doucette, as he got ready to leave after breakfast on the balcony. 'I'm sure the hotel will lend you one.'

Monsieur Pamplemousse glanced up at the sky. He shook his head. He had seen the Soleil d'Or's umbrellas. Enormous steel-framed contraptions. Like the hotel itself, they were a throw-back to the thirties; built to last. It would be an added encumbrance. Besides, he would sooner get wet than run the risk of being struck by lightning.

Nevertheless, having waved goodbye to Doucette, he headed for the reception desk. There were a few more questions he wanted to ask.

'*Les Russes?*' The *concierge* was as non-committal as the remains of Monsieur Pamplemousse's investment allowed; giving value for money, but no more, and no less.

The Russians had taken a suite at the hotel for the month of June to be near their daughter. 'Come the beginning of July, when the schools break up,' he gave a shrug.

'Who knows?'

'One has to accept the world as it is, Monsieur. Not as one would like it to be.'

One might also argue they are only carrying on a tradition. In the old days the Grand Dukes used to flock to the Riviera to escape the ice and snow of the Russian winters.'

In other words, thought Monsieur Pamplemousse, if you are a hotelkeeper would you turn away such big spenders? If you were a *restaurateur* and people came in, ordered the most expensive dishes on the menu, drank the best wines, paid in cash – lavishly tipping all and sundry into the bargain, would you turn them away, tell them never to darken your doorway again? Nor, if the truth were told, would it be wise to do so.

It had been before his time, but in those days Paris had been full of white Russian taxi drivers fleeing from the Bolsheviks, although he would have been willing to bet they hadn't been made to feel quite so welcome.

Pommes Frites was ready and waiting, eager for a change of scene. In his opinion there was a limit to the number of times a dog could chase seagulls off a pier without losing face. As soon as his back was turned they appeared again. A walk with his master couldn't have happened at a better time.

Passing the row of shops on the way to the school, Monsieur Pamplemousse saw that the blacked out window he had noticed the previous evening belonged to a delicatessen; now offering a mouth-watering display of *charcuterie*.

Unable to resist going inside, he bought a *saucisson* for Pommes Frites to have with his lunch, along with some freshly-made black *boudin*. It would be some compensation for his having to make do with an inflatable kennel while they were on holiday; yet another exercise in conscience easing.

For some reason best known to himself, Pommes Frites seemed to be playing his cards close to his chest. Clearly something had been on his mind ever since they arrived.

More often than not when they were on their travels he shared his master's room, and it was hard to explain away those occasions when it wasn't possible. *Chiens interdit* signs he knew, but the small print on hotel brochures meant less than nothing to him. It would be a shame if he took it personally.

On the other hand, the *saucisson* in particular struck him as a good omen. It was a Bâton de Berger aux Noisettes from Justin Bridou. The picture on the label of a man wearing a beret and green jacket – he'd always assumed it was Monsieur Bridou himself, clearly a man of infinite wisdom when it came to the finer points of *charcuterie* – brought back memories of his time in the *Sûreté*. In those days it had been his preferred choice of a persuader on those occasions when information had to be extracted quickly and cleanly from people who, by the very nature of their calling, were reluctant to talk. Speaking personally, although they only weighed a mere 250g, he had found them to be even more effective as a blunt instrument than the well-worn Paris telephone directory favoured by many of his colleagues; particularly as the latter also lacked the addition of *noisettes*.

There was a noticeable spring to Pommes Frites' step too as they resumed their walk. The *saucisson* happened to be one of his favourites, although for vastly different reasons.

The *boules* area was already occupied and he waited patiently while his master stopped for a moment or two to watch a game in progress. Then, as they drew near the school, he set off on a quick tour round the car park in order to make one last check-up on various trails before finally committing them to memory. If it was going to rain – and even without the benefit of a radio in his kennel there was little doubt in his own mind that they hadn't long to wait before it did, then any lingering smells would soon be washed away.

Pausing again at the school gates Monsieur Pamplemousse looked up and registered for the first time an almost windowless five-story tower block attached to one side of the building. There was a complicated array of aerials on the roof. He had no idea of their purpose, but it didn't surprise him; they went with all the sophisticated technology he had seen the previous evening. Once again, though, it was clearly a case of no expense spared.

He could hear music issuing from the main hall: a reprise of "Gee, Officer Krumpke". It hadn't occurred to him that the school would be mounting more than one performance of the musical.

Had his mind not been firmly fixed on other things, the music mistress in particular, Monsieur Pamplemousse might well have noticed that in the short time since they had left their hotel the cumulus clouds had given way to a mountainous development of dark-based cumulonimbus.

If the weather forecaster had been in attendance he would undoubtedly have waxed lyrical on the subject; explaining that technically the change had been brought about through a body of warm, moist air rising from the sea, leaving behind an area of low pressure. And since nature abhors a vacuum, the surrounding air rushing in to fill the space had formed a rapidly accelerating upward current.

Back at the hotel, as a wind began to develop, the boatman lashed his craft more firmly to its moorings, waiters hastily dismantled the few sun-shades they had put up, and of their own accord sea-gulls made for the safety of a sheltered cove.

In the school car park Pommes Frites began chasing dried leaves as they rose into the air like hundreds of awakening butterflies, while all around him a myriad of tiny creatures made a concerted dash for safety.

Certainly, had Monsieur Pamplemousse chanced to look even higher, beyond the array of aerials, he couldn't have failed to notice that an anvil-shaped cloud had developed overhead. A more fanciful observer of the passing scene might have suggested it had simply been biding its time until he arrived.

The first intimation of there being anything seriously amiss came as he was about to ring the doorbell to announce his presence. There was a blinding flash of light as an avalanche of electrons discharged itself from the cloud and headed in a laser-like beam towards the earth at a speed of 300,000 kilometres a second. For a brief moment the grey-green leaves of the ancient olive tree behind him – the very same tree where Pommes Frites had been waiting for them the previous evening – seemed almost transfixed, as though it had received a mighty blow.

It took a lot to destroy an olive tree, and he would put his money on its gnarled branches surviving the shock, but he wouldn't have fancied the chances of anyone sheltering beneath it.

Bouncing straight back up again, compressing the air as it went, the flash created a sound wave, which moments later announced its presence with an ear-splitting clap of thunder.

Hardly had Monsieur Pamplemousse recovered from the first shock-wave than a second flash struck the tower block. Ignoring the array of multi-faceted omni-directional aerials, possibly through being spoilt for choice, it singled out a small and relatively inoffensive satellite dish, and in a split second left it hanging from its mast, a blackened ruin.

Another horrendous crack of thunder, louder even than the first, left Monsieur Pamplemousse thanking his lucky stars he hadn't been carrying an umbrella.

Almost immediately the door was flung open and his ears were assailed by girlish screams as the entire school orchestra, the majority having abandoned their instruments, pushed him to one side as they streamed past, heading towards the surrounding woods. They were closely followed by the music mistress, still clutching her baton; then by members of the junior school and their attendants.

Throwing caution to the wind, Monsieur Pamplemousse dashed after them. '*Non! Non!*' He gesticulated towards the olive tree, hoping to demonstrate in as potent a way possible the danger they were in. 'You must stay where you are... *ici*... here... *à la belle étoile!*... out in the open!'

It seemed for a moment as though his words were falling on deaf ears, but another flash of lightning, followed by the inevitable clap of thunder brought them all skidding to a halt.

Suddenly uncomfortably aware they were hanging onto his every word and that the worst possible scenario would be to have the entire school population carbonised before his very eyes, he drew on a recent article that had appeared in l'Escargot.

'*Disperser-vous,*' he ordered, pointing towards the open play area. 'It is necessary that you should present the least possible surface towards the sky... *faites comme moi*. Watch me!'

The article had been written by one of his colleagues, Glandier, who had been born and brought up in the Savoy mountains, so he should know how to survive a thunderstorm if anyone did.

What was it he had said? Having found a suitable spot out in the open, bend over and touch the ground with your hands. Never stand with your feet apart lest lightning, having struck one leg, travels back down to earth via the other. Monsieur Pamplemousse shivered as he recalled the description of what might happen en route should the worst happen. Glandier was never one to mince his words.

Suddenly aware that all had gone quiet, Monsieur Pamplemousse looked up and gazed at the serried ranks of *derrières* spread out with almost mathematical precision in front of him. Tallest at the front, smallest at the back, their heads touching the ground, the only exception – a pastiche of the famous Hitchcock shot of a Wimbledon tennis match, when all but one of the crowd were watching the progress of the ball – was the girl he had last seen at breakfast. She was staring at him as though she could hardly believe her eyes.

He hastily turned his attention to the others. Possibly his

instructions had lost a little in translation, but from where he was positioned it looked as though the more enthusiastic of the senior pupils were intent on presenting the largest possible surface to the heavens rather than the least. Although lightning was said never to strike the same spot twice, were he the God Thor he might be tempted to make an exception in a number of cases.

Almost as though carrying out a preliminary reconnaissance, a gust of wind passed along the nearest row, lifting skirts which were doing little enough as it was to render more than a token service towards preserving their wearers' decorum.

Spotting the music mistress almost immediately in front of him, Monsieur Pamplemousse averted his gaze momentarily, then hesitated. The technician in him rose to the surface. Her *derrière*, would make admirable foreground interest: living, breathing proof, if proof were needed, that a curve is always more interesting than the straight line. Its juxtaposition with the military precision of the rows of girls would make it doubly so.

Would Cartier-Bresson, he asked himself, have wasted such a golden opportunity? The answer, of course, was a resounding NO! The great man may have had his faults - who didn't? – but indecision was not one of them. The precious moment of truth captured in an instant and frozen for all time had always been his particular forté.

Faced with such a unique, not say golden opportunity, he would have been hot-footing it to the nearest darkroom by now.

Likewise that other great practitioner of the art, Doisneau, who always maintained that the moment someone said "don't move" the picture was ruined.

As a potential subject for the front cover of l'Escargot it was a must: a welcome change from endless studies of lobster pots and *bœuf en croute*.

Thankful for the rising wind which drowned both the

sound of the shutter and the whirr of the high-speed motor-wind, Monsieur Pamplemousse got through half the remaining 34 exposures of his film in just under four seconds.

Another blinding flash caused him to release the button and he seized the opportunity to take up another position before pressing it again.

As soon as the rest of the film had been exposed and the automatic rewind had stopped he set about reloading the camera as fast as he could. Now that he had embarked on the operation he was determined to make the most of it.

While he was concentrating on the task in hand, Pommes Frites trotted into view, stopped dead in his tracks and gave a double take. Although over the years he had grown used to his master's peccadilloes, this was something on scale he had never encountered before, and for a moment or two he gazed in awe at the scene laid out before him. It was, although of course he had no reason to be aware of the fact, even more spectacular than the tableau involving a group of chorus girls at the *Folies*, which had been the cause of Monsieur Pamplemousse's enforced early retirement from the Paris *Sûreté*.

Blithely unaware of the widely-held superstition that a dog's tail can act as a lightning conductor, he raised his own appendage to its full height. Relying on the good offices of St. Hubert, the patron saint of bloodhounds, he then tempted fate still further by wagging it furiously as he took up a position at the end of the front line. Sad to say, his moment of euphoria was destined to be short-lived.

While the storm was breaking, millions of tiny water droplets condensed from the rising current of moist air had not been idle. Having found themselves floating aimlessly in space, they gradually coalesced into larger drops, joined up with others, then formed themselves into hailstones. At which point, obeying yet another of nature's immutable laws – the one which states that what goes up must eventually come down, and to the accompaniment of renewed peels of thunder, the Heavens opened and they began falling from the sky with ever increasing speed.

Monsieur Pamplemousse hastily closed the camera back, slipped the fully exposed film into his jacket pocket, and put the *boudin* under his hat for safe keeping. He was about set to work again when, without warning, he was knocked flying by a sudden blow to the head.

Momentarily convinced he had been struck by lightning, he staggered forward and while trying to recover his balance glimpsed a figure looming behind him.

A quick backward kick with the sharp edge of his right shoe produced a satisfactory howl of pain. As his assailant spun round he managed – more by luck than judgement – to land a second kick to the Achilles tendon. Having regained the initiative, he seized the opportunity to make a grab for Pommes Frites' *saucisson* and aimed a third blow towards an exposed muscle at the base of the man's neck.

Recovering his balance, he automatically adopted a defensive karate horse stance – feet wide apart, arms at the side, forearms outstretched and fists clenched – and gazed down at the figure sprawled on the ground in front of him while trying to get his breath back. It was quite like old times.

The next attack came when he least expected it, although a flicker in the man's eyes should have forewarned him. A second blow to the head, again from behind, but this time harder than the first, sent him reeling.

Everything seemed to be happening at once, but in a kind of slow-motion montage, almost as though he were swimming out of his depth. As the water began closing about him he was dimly aware of shouts and screams, and of someone wrenching the camera from his grasp. From somewhere else a long way away, came the sound of a dog barking. Then, as his head made contact with something hard, everything began to dissolve and he lost consciousness.

The kiss of life

When nature bestows one of its manifold bounties on a living creature, more often than not it exacts a price, presumably with an eye to preserving the inherent balance of things. So it was that Pommes Frites shared a trait common to most bloodhounds: his unique sense of smell was counterbalanced by a distinct lack of what an optician would call 20/20 vision. Nor, since nothing is perfect, was he equipped with a rear-view mirror and it was several moments before he realised what was going on behind his back.

Having received an early blow on the end of his nose from one of the hailstones, he not unnaturally attributed the girlish screams rising from all around him to the fact that others were suffering a similar fate, albeit on target areas rather larger, if not more sensitive than his own. That being so, he turned his mind to other things. What, for example, was the man hovering on the far side of the play area doing? Instinct told him that he was up to no good.

It wasn't until, looking over his shoulder, his gaze happened to alight on a familiar pair of shoes protruding from the bottom of an untidy pile of bodies some distance away, that he gave his second double-take in as many minutes. Even then his immediate reaction was one of patient tolerance. Clearly his master was up to his tricks again.

Several more seconds went by before it dawned on him that the legs to which the shoes were attached were the only ones among an assortment of threshing limbs which weren't actually moving. They hadn't, in fact, stirred since he first spotted them. It looked for all the world as though his master was about to be borne away in triumph by a swarm of giant female soldier ants.

Several girls seemed to be fighting to take possession of an arm; some, clearly unable to get as close to the action as they would have liked, stood helplessly by, wringing their hands in desperation. Others were running round and round in circles wailing, while two of the more enterprising girls appeared to be doing their level best to divest the inert figure of his clothing – his shirt was already half off.

Even as he watched, he saw another, this time larger than the rest, place her lips against his master's, as though about to wish him goodbye before he set off on a long journey. If the time and energy she was putting into the act had any bearing on the matter, it was a journey from which he was unlikely to return.

Ignoring a rapidly stifled cry from somewhere nearby, and in order to make up for lost time, Pommes Frites hastened to investigate the matter.

On closer inspection, even though by now the hailstones were rapidly turning to rain, it struck him that his master didn't look entirely unhappy with the turn of events. Indeed, not to put too fine a point on it, anyone less charitably inclined than Pommes Frites might have suggested the reverse to be true. Still clasping the *saucisson* in his right hand, he appeared to be perfectly content for the time being to lie exactly where he had fallen. There was, thought Pommes Frites, no accounting for tastes.

Having detected a barely perceptible sign, the merest flicker of an eyelid – the Food Inspector's equivalent of a Film Director's classic "take five" – indicating that for the time being his services weren't required, Pommes Frites pricked up his ears. He turned his attention instead to the distant sound of trampling feet somewhere beyond the shrubbery, and without further ado he abandoned plan "A" and set off in hot pursuit.

Pommes Frites was never very happy leaving Monsieur Pamplemousse on his own.

It wasn't so much that he didn't trust his master to look after himself. It was *other people*, and as far as he could see there were quite a lot of those around who were acting suspiciously.

One way and another he'd had a busy time over the past two days; following trails, retracing not only his own steps, but others almost too numerous to mention. During the course of his perambulations he had collected a number of items that were now safely stored beneath an old blanket at the back of his kennel. He felt sure they would be of interest to his master when the time was ripe.

But for now it was a case of first things first, and Pommes Frites knew where his priorities lay.

Seeing the tail end of his friend and mentor disappear into the bushes at high speed, Monsieur Pamplemousse relaxed.

Having woken at the very moment when the kiss of life was being applied, it had taken him several moments of close study to confirm that it really was the music mistress who was astride him and not some winged messenger sent down from on high to render first aid. As for the girl who was feeling his pulse, she was pressing so hard, if she didn't watch out it would stop altogether.

'Atkreevat...'

He had no idea what the mistress was saying – it sounded more like double Dutch than anything he had come across before – but the phrase "whispering sweet nothings" took on an entirely new meaning as a warm tongue entered his mouth, forcing it open still further.

'Sheerokeey kaka laye...' Yielding to the pressure, he felt a scented draught of air enter his mouth. It wasn't a perfume he immediately recognised.

'Wide... wider... *toute grande.*'

Feeling others tugging at his arms and legs, Monsieur Pamplemousse wondered for a moment if perhaps he wasn't in some heavenly massage parlour, a kind of staging post where candidates selected for even greater delights were prepared for their final exams... Apart from obvious reasons of convenience there was no guarantee that French would be the chosen language. Although, logically, of course...

'*Sapristi!*' He jumped as he felt a wet hand on his heart.

Light dawned. Initially the girl must have been speaking to him in Russian. So much for his theories on national differences. On the other hand...as the tip of her tongue made yet another exploratory sortie, he lay back and considered the matter.

She could have been living in France for so long she had absorbed the best characteristics of her adopted country. That must be it.

And if that were the case, then undoubtedly it was a marriage made in heaven. He glanced down. Doucette was right, as always. Confirmation of her theories regarding lack of support for the music mistress's *doudounes* was closer to hand than he would have dreamed possible. Doubly so, in fact; they were like two peaches, luscious and ripe for plucking. Memories of many a crescendo in "Gee, Officer Krupke" came flooding back. His involuntary sigh elicited renewed efforts on the part of his benefactress, and this time, feeling powerless to resist, he offered himself up to whatever fate might have in store. Indeed, it would have been churlish of him to act otherwise. These things were best left to the experts. Clearly, youthful though she was, the girl was experienced in matters of resuscitation, for he was already beginning to feel concrete evidence of the return to life.

Having closed both eyes in order to gain the full benefit of her ministrations, Monsieur Pamplemousse immediately opened one of them again – the one nearest the shrubbery – as he heard the sound of something heavy approaching.

He was just in time to see Pommes Frites burst into view. He was wearing his pleased expression, as well he might, for the stolen Leica was firmly clasped in his capacious mouth. Indeed, with the lens pointing straight ahead and his jowls overlapping either side of its body, he looked for all the world as though he could be about to swallow a giant marble. Either that or he was sprouting a third eye.

'*Asseyez-vous*!' Monsieur Pamplemousse rapped out the word of command.

'*Qu'est-ce que c'est?*'

The mistress's cry of alarm as she looked round and saw Pommes Frites crouching down only a few feet away, was echoed by all and sundry.

'*Ne vous effrayez pas.* Do not worry. There is no cause for alarm.'

For a second or two it crossed Monsieur Pamplemousse's mind to feign a relapse, but seeing the look on Pommes Frites' face he hastily decided against the idea. Expectancy had been replaced by something else; it was hard to tell what. Anxiety? Fear? The triumphant look had vanished; the eyes had lost their shine and his face had taken on a mournful expression. Perhaps, given the combined size of the camera and its winder attachment he was about to throw up?

Then again, was it the look of a dog who was planning some kind of rescue operation? If so – and Monsieur Pamplemousse certainly wouldn't put it past him – who knew where it would end? The *pompiers* might well become involved, and if it turned out to be the same lot he'd encountered the previous morning they might feel inclined to make up for their lost football. He could imagine their whoops of joy as they pounced on him.

The matter was unexpectedly resolved as Pommes Frites suddenly leapt to his feet and disappeared into the shrubbery as fast as his legs would carry him.

The truth of the matter was he had been feeling a faint vibration coming from the object in his mouth. And accompanying the vibration had been the sound of ticking.

Having once, during the Algerian troubles, spent a period with the Bomb Disposal Squad, during which time he had been trained to search for explosive devices, he was well versed on the subject of bombs, and he was convinced he'd been holding one in his mouth.

Torn between wanting to receive his master's approbation for retrieving his property and getting rid of it as quickly as possible, it didn't take him long to decide on the latter course.

Even during the few seconds he had spent debating the subject, the whirring had ceased. So, too, had the ticking. In his experience that was never a good sign. Whenever ticking had stopped on the course his instructors had made a run for it, calling on him to follow. Almost always it had been followed by an explosion. Once with particularly dire results.

Already suffering pangs of remorse for leaving his master unattended in his hour of need, Pommes Frites decided he needed to take the object as far away as possible and bury it, preferably in sand. That was another thing he had learned on his course. Sandbags had come in for a lot of use. And if sandbags were well thought of, then how much better must it be to bury a suspect object in somewhere like a beach?

Destined to go unrecorded, Pommes Frites' act of bravery was on a par with that of a Newfoundland dog named Gander V.C., who was blown to pieces while removing a hand grenade which had been thrown at a group of wounded Canadian riflemen during the war with Japan. It was simply yet another case of a dog having to do what a dog had to do where the safety of its master was concerned.

Silence followed his departure. The music mistress rose to her feet and Monsieur Pamplemousse did his best to follow suit.

'You are all right, no?' said the girl anxiously. 'I thought for one moment...'

'I think I shall live,' said Monsieur Pamplemousse simply.

'I hope so.' She hesitated, suddenly shy as she caught him staring at the thin, rain-soaked dress clinging to her body. Then she looked up at the sky. 'The storm has passed.'

It was true. Already there were gaps in the clouds.

'You are wet, Katya… You should have a hot bath as soon as possible.'

'You know my name!' For a moment she looked confused.

'I looked it up in the programme yesterday evening.'

She looked pleased. 'You enjoyed the performance? You are wanting to come again?'

Monsieur Pamplemousse shook his head and explained why he was there.

No, there had been nothing for him and she was sure she would have known if there had been. She had been the last to leave that night.

As they said goodbye it struck him that her handshake was full of unspoken thoughts, but that was probably wishful thinking on his part. Her mind was probably already on the evening's performance. Wanting to catch up on lost rehearsal time.

She hesitated. 'Please to close your eyes.'

He obeyed, and a moment later felt her dabbing at his mouth, then she placed something in his hand and gave it a squeeze.

'Now you may open them.'

Looking down, he found himself holding a tiny white handkerchief, embroidered in one corner with red roses surrounding the letter K. It felt warm to the touch. It was also covered in lipstick.

'Please to keep it. It is to bring you luck and to wish you safe keeping.'

Half turning in order to undo a back pocket in his trousers, when Monsieur Pamplemousse looked up again she was gone.

By the time he reached the shops the sun was shining. Steam was already rising from the road. In places the tarmac surface had completely dried out.

Half expecting to find Pommes Frites waiting for him, he hesitated outside the photographic shop, wondering whether or not to risk leaving the film for processing.

Catching sight of his reflection in the window, he decided against it. He looked a mess; jacket and trousers crumpled almost out of recognition, button-down shirt ripped apart, lipstick on what was left of the collar.

Far better to send it off to Headquarters by the fastest possible means. Let Trigaux work his magic printing up the negatives. He, too, had entered the digital age, updating his darkroom with the latest high-tech equipment.

Slinking into the hotel, he managed to escape the eyes of those on duty at the main desk who were busy with pre-noon departures. Making a detour round the dinner gong, he avoided the lift, and mounted the stairs to his room two at a time.

Hastily removing his damp clothes he dumped them in a pile on the floor, luxuriated for a few minutes under a warm shower, then donned a dressing gown while planning his next move.

First things first. Having found a plastic laundry bag in the bathroom cupboard, he ran his finger down the list of options alongside the telephone, dialled 6 for the valet service and gave his room number.

Turning on the radio he caught the tail end of an up-dated weather forecast. '...it has rearranged itself. The back-packer in the sky has rolled up his sleeping bag and is on his way to pastures new. It may be wise to give him a head start though...'

A quick glance out of the balcony window confirmed that life was back to normal. The bay was already alive with water skiers making up for lost time; tables laid ready for lunch awaited their return.

It was like that on the coast; weather changed rapidly and the bad was soon forgotten.

The beach area was filling up. There was no sign of either Doucette or Mrs. Pickering. They must still be in Antibes. Mr. Pickering, pipe in mouth, was standing in the water with his trousers rolled up, gazing back at the hotel. Todd was nowhere to be seen. Presumably he was busy exporting or importing whatever it was that passed through his hands to make a show of things. If, indeed, he even bothered to do that. Nor was there any sign of the Russians.

Pommes Frites went past looking pleased with himself. Even from a distance Monsieur Pamplemousse could see his paws were covered in wet sand; rather as though he had been digging. His heart sank.

An unfamiliar muffled ringing sound took him back into the room. It was a moment or two before he realised it was coming from inside Le Guide's case and was another of Monsieur Leclercq's recent innovations – the mobile phone. That said, he detected the hand of Madame Grante in Accounts behind the move. She was always grumbling about the use of hotel telephones with their vast mark-up. Given the number of calls back to base the Inspectors normally made during the course of a year, she probably had a point.

Searching out the Nokia, he activated it.

'There you are at last, Aristide.' It was Monsieur Leclercq. 'Enjoying what you photographers call f32 weather, I trust. Ah, how I envy you. No doubt you are making good use of the haze filter.'

'It has been more f2 than f32, *Monsieur*,' said Monsieur Pamplemousse gloomily. 'As for the haze filter, I am afraid that and the spare lenses are all I have left.'

'What are you saying, Pamplemousse?' barked the Director. 'Don't tell me you left the camera body in Paris. I know this is meant to be a holiday, but staff working for Le Guide are expected to be on duty at all times; the contents of their issue case on hand *jour et nuit*, ready to cope with any emergency. There is no point in your having one otherwise.'

'I'm afraid the camera was stolen, *Monsieur*.'

'Stolen?' repeated the Director. 'From your room? You have reported the matter, of course.'

'No, *Monsieur*. It wasn't in the hotel at the time. I was

attacked from behind while taking some pictures for the Staff Magazine.'

'From behind? Did you manage to catch a glimpse of the miscreant?'

'I would recognise him at once if ever we meet again, *Monsieur*.' He forebore to say there had been two. It would only complicate the issue.

'Excellent. I trust you have been in touch with the police. Photofit pictures can be made based on your description. I will get Veronique to check on the serial number of the camera.'

'I can save your secretary the trouble,' said Monsieur Pamplemousse. 'Pommes Frites retrieved it for me.'

'Good. Good. *Excellent!* What would you do without him? What would *we* do without him come to that? I hope it is still in working order?'

'Unfortunately...' Monsieur Pamplemousse hesitated, choosing his words with care. 'I have no means of knowing. He ran off with it.'

'Ran off with it?' repeated the Director. 'Did you not call him back?'

'I was in no position to,' said Monsieur Pamplemousse, hoping Monsieur Leclercq wouldn't ask him why. 'The thing is, he has hidden it somewhere.'

'Hidden it? That is not possible. In any case, why would he do that?'

'I'm sure he had his reasons, *Monsieur*. He probably felt·he was acting for the best.'

'As an ex-member of the Paris Sûreté, highly trained in sniffing things out, he should experience no difficulty in finding it again. You must order him to.'

'It is not as easy as that, *Monsieur*. It will be against his nature. When it comes to hiding things, his lips are sealed. That, too, was part of his training.'

'A very negative aspect, if you want my opinion,' said the Director crossly. 'If that is the situation, then you must do everything in your power to unseal them before someone else finds it.'

'Cap d'Antibes covers a large area, Monsieur. It is full of nooks and crannies. He may even…' Monsieur Pamplemousse took a deep breath. *'Par exemple,* it is possible he may even have buried it in the sand.'

'Buried it in the sand?' While the Director appeared to be fighting the onset of a mild attack of apoplexy, Monsieur Pamplemousse seized the opportunity to adjust the volume of the earpiece in a downward direction. 'What if the tide comes in before it is found?'

'Fortunately, Monsieur, there is no worry on that score. As Monsieur will be aware the Medit…'

'This is no time for complacency, Pamplemousse,' boomed the Director. 'The fact that the Mediterranean is tideless is small consolation. I shudder to think what effect prolonged exposure to salt water will have.'

'With respect, Monsieur, Pommes Frites is only obeying his instincts.'

'That, Pamplemousse, is not how Madame Grante will see it. She will not be pleased.'

'Madame Grante has not been hit over the head…' Monsieur Pamplemousse stifled a desire to suggest that such things could be arranged. 'Fortunately I happened to have some *boudin* under my hat and that softened the blow.'

There was a moment's silence while the Director digested the latest piece of information. When he next spoke his tone was unusually mild.

'Forgive me, Aristide. I had no idea it was that serious. It is probably a foolish question, but I must ask it all the same. Was there any particular reason why you were carrying a quantity of *boudin* inside you hat, other than for protection against possible blows about the head?'

'There was a bad storm, Monsieur. I was keeping it dry for Pommes Frites.'

'Ah, very sensible.' The Director sounded relieved. 'I have

never partaken of a wet *boudin*, but I imagine it would be somewhat unpalatable. Not a pleasant experience. One would search in vain for a suitable recipe in *Larousse Gastronomique*.'

'Not only that, *Monsieur*. I was fortunate enough to have a *Bâton de Berger aux noisettes* with me. It is something else Pommes Frites is partial to. My assailant did not make good his escape without first having felt its full weight behind him. In my days with the *Sûreté* I often made use of it when it came to eliciting information from those who had the misfortune to be suffering a temporary loss of memory. The *noisettes* were particularly efficacious in restoring it. They added a certain body…'

'I do not wish to know that,' broke in the Director. 'Nor, I imagine, would the manufacturers. "As used by the Paris *Sûreté* during their interrogations" is hardly the kind of endorsement they would wish to see appearing on their labels. Nor would the phrase "a sure cure for amnesia" do much for their sales figures.'

'It sounds even worse in German…' Monsieur Pamplemousse felt honour bound to defend his late employers. 'In German it is called *Puur Vareknsworst Met Hazelnoten*. The other advantage was that you could collect coupons off the label and for two coupons plus 25 francs receive in return a disposable camera.'

'I hope you are not suggesting that as a means of replacing the Leica,' barked the Director. 'I doubt if Madame Grante will see it that way.'

There was a pause, during which Monsieur Pamplemousse thought he detected the sound of fingers drumming.

'I am beginning to feel, Pamplemousse,' continued Monsieur Leclercq at long last, 'that your time in the *Sûreté* – and this applies to both you and Pommes Frites – was not always well spent.

'Gross misuse of *Bâtons de Berger*. Training dogs to withhold vital information. It is a wonder to me you both lasted as long as you did. Really, it is most disappointing. I can only suggest you fill in a P37B, "Loss of Property during the Hours of Duty" form, whilst the unhappy incident is still fresh in your mind. Please let me have it back as soon as possible.'

'*Oui, Monsieur.*' Monsieur Pamplemousse settled for the soft soap approach. 'I am already planning to send off a reel of film I took during the storm. I can put the form in with it.'

'You took some snaps? Before the camera was stolen?'

'*Oui, Monsieur.* It was one of the most spectacular displays of pyrotechnics I have ever witnessed. It was a case of seizing the opportunity while it lasted. Fortunately, having reloaded the camera with a fresh film before it was stolen, I still have the first cassette. I am hoping it contains something suitable for L'Escargot. If *Monsieur* should decide to go public, it is worth remembering the annual awards for the magazine cover of the year are coming up, and it could be worth entering. To win such a coveted award with the very first issue would be an enormous feather in our cap.'

It did the trick. Monsieur Leclercq's explosions rarely lasted for long, and he was clearly excited at the thought.

'This is excellent news, Aristide. There is no time to be lost. I will arrange for a courier service to pick it up from the hotel as soon as possible. If it reaches Nice airport in good time it could be put on a plane for Orly. Trigaux should have it for processing by late this afternoon. I will make sure he lets me have the results as soon as possible.'

'*Oui, Monsieur.*'

'And Aristide…'

'*Monsieur?*'

'In the meantime I will prepare the ground with Madame Grante. Perhaps a little bouquet of her favourite flowers marked "A Present from the Riviera" would not be out of place?'

'As you wish, *Monsieur.*'

Knowing Madame Grante of old, he felt certain such a

gesture would be singularly out of place, particularly if he tried to claim it on expenses. Her suspicions would be roused straight away, but he had no wish to disturb the note of tranquillity that terminated the conversation.

It wasn't until after he had pressed the OFF key that he realised he had failed to mention anything about his lack of success in picking up the painting, still less his fears as to why that was. On the other hand, Monsieur Leclercq hadn't brought the subject up either. Perhaps he had been feeling distracted too.

Feeling in need of a stiff drink, he opened the refrigerator door, studied the row of miniature bottles in the rack, and settled on a vodka; a double vodka with ice would be admirable. In the circumstances even Madame Grante couldn't begrudge him a medicinal pick-me-up.

Settling himself down at a small table near the window, he opened up the lap-top and powered it. It would take him all his time to marshal his report into some kind of logical order.

Putting off the evil moment, squaring his conscience with the excuse that it would help clear his mind, he set the computer up for a game of Free Cell. All the aces were along the top row, which in his experience meant there wasn't a hope of getting it out, so he decided to make it the best out of four.

There was now no question in his mind – he had struck a run of bad luck in all directions. Ten minutes later, weary of all the warning pings and bells and in a worse mood than when he started, he idly switched into the Smart Capture mode, hoping that might do the trick by triggering off a few thoughts. It was the electronic equivalent of sharpening pencils.

Hearing the sound of a key being inserted into a lock behind him, Monsieur Pamplemousse rotated the lens and watched on the screen as the top half of the door slowly opened, then closed again. Reaching forward, he gently rotated the pod, zooming in at the same time until the head and shoulders of a man came into view. Whoever it was, he appeared to be watching him intently.

Mindful of a sophisticated version of the original Minitel service which provided an escape route for those who were caught watching the so-called "pink" services (known as the "my wife is coming" button, it replaced porn with a table of meaningless statistics), he returned to the games mode.

Bracing himself before the other had a chance to make the first move, Monsieur Pamplemousse leapt to his feet, pushing the chair aside at the same time, and having closed the gap between the two of them in a couple of strides, gripped the intruder by his collar and tie.

'*Cochon…! Salud…! Maquereau…! Enfant de putain…! Débile mentale…! Imbécile…!*' Effectively punctuating each word by slamming his victim against the wall, it wasn't until he found himself running short of expletives that he realised the man's cheeks were glistening.

'Please…'

'*Sapristi!*' Expecting to hear Russian rather than English, it took him by surprise. 'I don't know who you are or what you want,' he said, loosening his grip, 'but I never, *ever* want to see you again. And I warn you here and now, if I so much as catch a glimpse of you in the far distance I shall make sure you will regret it for the rest of your days. And when I have finished with you, others will begin. Now get out of here and don't come back.'

With that, he flung the door open with his free hand and hurled the intruder into the corridor. As the man landed in a heap, he traced an imaginary line left to right across his forehead with the forefinger of his right hand, palm facing downwards, in the classic *J'en ai ras le bol* gesture.

'I have had it up to here with you people!'

Pausing only to reverse the card on the door handle so that it read DO NOT DISTURB, he slammed the door shut behind him, and having made sure the security latch was firmly in place, returned to the table.

Breathing heavily after his exertions, Monsieur Pamplemousse flopped into the chair. It was always the same: bottle things up for too long and when the cork eventually popped under the pressure, all the pent-up frustrations came out with a rush...

He stared at his vodka glass. A moment ago it had been full. Now it was lying across the keyboard – empty! Upending it, a drop no larger than a budgerigar's *larme* – certainly smaller than the man's teardrops – clung suspended from the rim for a brief moment, then landed on the table beside him. Upending the lap-top produced a similar result. A tiny smidgen of liquid trickled its way down the keyboard, winding a path in and out of the keys before joining the first drop.

He barely had time to read the ominous phrase YOU HAVE PERFORMED AN ILLEGAL OPERATION before the picture faded and a metallic female voice uttered the dreaded words: "Your battery is running low".

Searching out the mains adapter, he powered the machine from a wall socket, but the screen remained resolutely blank. He tried shaking it, but there was not a bleep to be heard.

It was all he needed!

With the basic operating instructions contained in the HELP section of the programme only available when the laptop was working, he upended a large envelope that had come with it. Searching through a mass of documents hoping to find the usual world-wide list of main dealers, he drew a blank. All he found was a sheet of paper torn from an exercise book with the words **EN CAS D'URGENCE** scrawled across the top. Below it was written a telephone number. Once again there was something familiar about the writing. It could have been the same as that on the address of the antique dealer in Nice, but he couldn't be sure and anyway he had thrown that away.

He reached for his mobile. It was worth a try.

Pommes Frites gazed at a strange object, not unlike an elongated black dog biscuit, lying on the sand.

It was getting near lunch time and he had been hanging about outside the hotel in the hope of drawing his master's attention to the fact, when it had come flying out of an upstairs window and landed right by his feet.

Having circled it several times, he crouched down on his stomach, wormed his way forward, and gave a tentative sniff. A quick chew confirmed the fact that whatever it was, it certainly wasn't edible, but he recognised one thing straight away: the scent of his master.

And if his master had thrown it out of his window, it could mean only one thing. He wanted to get rid of it as quickly as possible. A ringing noise coming from somewhere inside it only served to emphasise the urgency of the matter. It was another thing he had learned on his course.

Being already in a disposing-of-bombs mode that morning, it didn't take him long to reach a decision. Unable to see a bucket of water anywhere close by, he did the next best thing. Once again risking life and limb, he picked the object up in his mouth and dunked it in the sea.

Having successfully stopped the ringing, he took it back to his kennel to join his other trophies before settling down on the beach again to await his master's pleasure.

Meanwhile, unaware of the dramas taking place outside his window, and temporarily deprived of his mobile, Monsieur Pamplemousse picked up the house phone and dialled 6.

Having waited a full two minutes he tried again. When there was still no reply he replaced the handset.

It was back to basics. Wearily, he added a comment to a growing list of items on the back of an old envelope.

There were days when an Inspector's lot was not a happy one. One thing was certain; if the Hôtel au Soleil carried on like this is would be losing its d'Or appendage long before the next edition of Le Guide was due out.

One of your derrières *is missing*

Reaching for his napkin, Monsieur Pamplemousse dabbed furiously at a large black lump on his right knee. It was all he needed to round off the day. His suit was in a bad enough state as it was without being spattered by a mixture of black olives, anchovies and olive oil.

Having left home in a hurry, he had omitted to pack a spare pair of trousers. At least he had brought his lightweight jacket with him, otherwise he would have felt conspicuous alongside the others: Doucette in the dress she kept for "special occasions", Mrs. Pickering, looking elegant in a white dress and Hermès scarf, Mr. Pickering hardly less so in grey trousers and a dark blue blazer.

'I believe French chalk is very good for absorbing oil stains,' said Mrs. Pickering.

'It will need to deal with many other things as well,' said Monsieur Pamplemousse gloomily. 'This version of *tapénade* has tuna fish mixed in. It helps reduce the saltiness. It also had capers and a hint of *pastis*. If you will excuse me…'

From an inside pocket, he produced his Cross pen and the envelope he had used for making notes on earlier in the day.

'You can't beat the tried and trusted methods,' said Mr. Pickering approvingly.

'Aristide is having trouble with his computer,' explained Doucette.

'I don't even have my notepad.' Monsieur Pamplemousse launched into a brief run-down of his troubles.

'You have my sympathy,' said Mr. Pickering. 'Computers can be quite petulant at times. They have a tendency to announce that you had committed a Fatal Error and refuse to do any more work without so much as a hint as to what you have done wrong.'

'In fairness,' said Monsieur Pamplemousse, 'I doubt if mine had come across vodka before.'

'It's the noises I can't stand,' said Mrs. Pickering. 'They are so smug and holier than thou when they're first switched on – full of sweeping chords and arpeggios. Then they get impatient and start pinging like a dripping tap.'

'That drives Aristide mad too,' agreed Doucette. 'My husband is a very patient man, but he does keep things bottled up. Then, when something snaps, it all comes out and he becomes a different person. It is like a thunderstorm. I hardly know him.'

Feeling himself on dangerous ground, Monsieur Pamplemousse tried to veer away from the subject.

'Talking of thunderstorms, please forgive the way I am dressed. I was caught out in the one we had this morning.'

'Another example of global warming,' said Mr. Pickering, applying some more of the anchovy paste to his toasted *pain de campagne*.

'Another example of being pig-headed,' said Doucette. 'I told him to take an umbrella.'

'You should be like Andrew,' said Mrs. Pickering. 'He never goes out without his wherever we are.'

'I did offer to iron Aristide's trousers,' broke in Doucette, 'but our room is like a workshop. There are flashing lights everywhere and all the wall sockets are taken up with battery chargers. I didn't even have one for my hairdrier.'

Mrs. Pickering murmured sympathetically. 'There are never enough sockets, and when you do find one it is never where you want it to be.'

'I'm afraid we English are partly to blame for that,' said Mr. Pickering. 'Ever since the Reverend Lewis Way instigated the laying out of the Promenade des Anglais in Nice, we have continued to leave our mark on this part of the world. Being much patronised by *les Anglais*, this hotel reflects old-fashioned values. In travel agents' brochures it is the kind of establishment where people don't actually stay, but take a sojourn. In most other respects it is hard to fault.'

'All except one.' Monsieur Pamplemousse glanced ruefully at his trousers. 'Twice this afternoon I rang for the valet service and nothing happened. If they are not careful the symbol of a steam iron will be missing from next year's guide.'

'In the circumstances,' said Mr. Pickering, 'it doesn't surprise me. But perhaps you haven't heard. Extraordinary business. Apparently one of the staff went to pick up a pair of trousers for cleaning and received a severe beating up for his pains. He arrived back downstairs a gibbering wreck and hasn't been seen since.'

Madame Pamplemousse shivered.

'Are you all right, Couscous?' Monsieur Pamplemousse put his arm protectively round her shoulder. 'Would you like me to fetch your pashmina?'

'No. I was just thinking how awful to be married to a beast like that. The man who attacked him, I mean. I shall be frightened to leave the room by myself from now on.'

'Do they have a record of the room number?' Monsieur Pamplemousse asked casually.

'Apparently not,' said Mr. Pickering. 'He was English, over here to learn French. It was his first day on duty, so he hadn't quite got into the swing of things. Anyway, it's too late now. At the rate he was going he's probably in Dover by now, vowing never to return.'

Monsieur Pamplemousse mentally breathed a sigh of relief.

'One way and another it's been quite a day,' said Mr. Pickering. 'I saw one of our Russians being whisked off to hospital this morning. Apart from having been hit about the head, he'd been bitten in a most unfortunate place. Then came the to-do over the laundry.'

'You'd think that while the police are looking into the other awful business with the body they would deal with it,' said Mrs. Pickering. 'The two things might be connected.'

Monsieur Pamplemousse shook his head. 'I'm afraid it isn't as simple as that. The problem with the laundry will be a matter for the local *Gendarmerie*. But since they are a military body under the control of the Army Minister and have no detectives, the case of the corpse will be handled by the nearest *Police Judiciaire*. They're controlled by the Ministry of the Interior and are very similar to the English City police. After that a *juge d'instruction* takes over.'

'I shall never get it straight,' said Mrs. Pickering.

'Loosely translated,' broke in Mr. Pickering, 'it means "examining magistrate" only in this case it's always a judge.'

'An even looser translation,' said Monsieur Pamplemousse, 'if you will excuse my saying so, is pain in the *derrière*. They are a law unto themselves. They virtually take over an investigation. They visit the scene of the crime, questioning everyone and everything. If you need a search warrant you have to get their permission first.'

'It's swings and roundabouts,' said Mr. Pickering. 'The Continental inquisitorial system may be slow, but at least by the time you get to court everything is sewn up. The weakness of our adversarial system, with counsel pitted against counsel, is that more often than not the man who can afford the best lawyer wins.

'Which reminds me. I haven't as yet seen anyone remotely resembling a magistrate, only a couple of what Todd would call "uniforms".'

It was true. Monsieur Pamplemousse had been out a good deal of the time, but everything seemed to have gone strangely quiet. Could one turn a blind eye to a limbless corpse being washed up on the shores of the Mediterranean? It wouldn't be the first time there had been shenanigans in that part of the world. It had reached its peak in the seventies when the Mayor of Nice, Jacques Médecin, had been forced to flee the country to Uruguay to escape imprisonment.

Before he had time to dwell on the matter, the first course arrived: *consommé Niçoise*. It was note-taking time again.

'Seeing our meeting by chance like this is a cause for celebration,' he said, 'I have taken the liberty of asking if the chef could prepare a selection of regional specialities. All in aid of research, of course.'

'Of course,' said Mr. Pickering drily. 'It's a hard job, but somebody has to do it.'

The dish was beyond reproach: clarified with egg whites, which had in turn been helped by acid from tomatoes, the liquid was so clear he could have put a ten franc coin at the bottom of the bowl and still read every word on it. It sparkled when he stirred it. There wasn't a trace of fat. Yet the taste of each and every one of the other ingredients was still there; beef…potatoes…green beans…

Monsieur Pamplemousse awarded it Le Guide's maximum points. 'The best of Nice cuisine tastes of what it is,' he said. 'Which is as it should be.'

He was on home ground and his feeling of wellbeing was increasing by the minute. It lasted until the pianist, who for some while had been wallowing in nostalgic rhythms of the twenties, suddenly broke off and segued into a spirited rendering of the theme from "Doctor Zhivago". Heads turned.

'Is the back of your neck burning?' asked Mr. Pickering. 'If it isn't, it ought to be. I don't think you are exactly flavour of the month with our Russian friends.'

'I don't see why they have taken against Aristide,' said Doucette. 'Just because he didn't buy one of their daughter's programmes.'

'I don't think it is as simple as that, Couscous,' said Monsieur Pamplemousse. 'I have a feeling that for whatever reason they are suspicious of me.'

While the table was being cleared prior to the arrival of the next course he seized the opportunity to steal a quick glance over his shoulder. Clearly something was wrong. If the pianist had been hoping for a little extra *pourboire* for his efforts he was wasting his time.

A whole sea bass arrived at their table and was presented.

Resting on a bed of watercress in a long oval dish, the upper skin had been removed to reveal flesh that was firm and white. It was garnished around the edge with slices of cucumber and lemon, interspersed with cherry tomatoes.

'It is this morning's catch, *Monsieur*,' said the Maître d', anticipating his question. 'It has been poached in a *court bouillon* of onions, carrots and celery.'

Placing the dish on a small serving table nearby, he began deftly cutting away portions of the upper side.

Monsieur Pamplemousse thanked him. 'We are privileged,' he murmured. 'Even in the South of France you can no longer guarantee fish have not been farmed in Calais with water warmed from some nuclear power station's cooling system.'

'Pumped full of antibiotics, no doubt,' said Mr. Pickering. 'It's the same with our salmon. And with lack of proper exercise, out goes the taste.'

'If I were a salmon,' said Mrs. Pickering, 'I'm not sure that I would want to swim all the way to Greenland and back simply because it would make me taste better.'

'It does help to put the colour in their cheeks,' said Mr. Pickering.

While the fish was being prepared for table, a bowl of freshly-made mayonnaise arrived. With it came a *mesclun* salad. Monsieur Pamplemousse identified lamb's lettuce, rocket, dandelions, wild chicory, and red and curly endive. It had been seasoned with olive oil.

The sommelier, whose name Monsieur Pamplemousse had discovered was Anouchka, materialised with a bottle of white Château de Crémat and held it up for inspection.

'May I?' Mr. Pickering leaned forward to examine the label.

'It is from Bellet, *Monsieur*,' said the girl. '330 metres up in the hills behind Nice. The vines are sheltered from the Mistral, but they benefit from long exposure to the sun. At the same time they are cooled by the sea breezes off the coast.'

Having tasted the wine, Monsieur Pamplemousse nodded his approval and she began to pour. 'They were first planted by the Phoenicians four centuries before the arrival of Christ. They say the wine can be aged for anything up to thirty years, but *alors*, it rarely has the chance. Most of it goes to the local restaurants long before then.'

'In that case we are doubly privileged,' said Mr. Pickering.

'What did you think of that?' he asked, as Anouchka went on her way.

'It makes me feel old,' said Monsieur Pamplemousse. 'In the Auvergne, when I was her age, we had red wine and we had white wine. We didn't ask too many questions about where it came from. Times change.'

'Well, here's to Todd, wherever he is,' said Mr. Pickering, raising his glass. 'He doesn't know what he's missing.'

Monsieur Pamplemousse reached for his pen again. The sea bass had been flavoured with herbs: bay leaves, thyme, fresh tarragon; and garnished with parsley. The mayonnaise was also lightly flavoured with tarragon, along with finely chopped parsley and chives. He reflected on the wine. It was perfectly chilled: cold, but not so cold that it masked the scent of wild flowers and lime blossom.

Under the table Pommes Frites licked his lips as a large portion of *boeuf en daube* arrived in a separate bowl, compliments of the chef. It disappeared before the others had even begun their fish. Monsieur Pamplemousse made another note.

'It's strange,' said Mrs. Pickering. 'We are supposed to be a nation of animal lovers, and yet how often do you see a dog eating in an English restaurant, or a Scottish one for that matter?'

'Our two nations are full of misconceptions about each other,' said Mr. Pickering.

'The popular perception used to be that if a Frenchman knocked an Englishman down with his car, the Englishman's first thought was to apologise – the Frenchman would then call him an imbecile for getting in the way. Nowadays it is more likely to be the other way round. You French have retained the little forms of politeness which we long ago gave up...'

He broke off as a minion from the front desk arrived bearing a note on a silver tray.

Headed URGENT, it was for Monsieur Pamplemousse. His heart sank as he read it.

'Not bad news, I hope?'

'Anything which interrupts a meal like this is bad news,' said Monsieur Pamplemousse.

'Must you, Aristide?' said Doucette, when she saw who it was from.

'I will take the call in our room. It will be easier in the long run.' The last person he wanted to speak to while he was in the middle of dinner was the Director. There would be no short cuts. On the other hand, clearly something must be amiss.

Having cleared his plate with as much haste as he could decently manage, Monsieur Pamplemousse made his way to the lift.

Monsieur Leclercq must have been waiting by the phone, for the receiver was picked up before the end of the second ring.

'There you are, Pamplemousse. At long last! Don't tell me your mobile has given up the ghost already. I have been trying to reach you all afternoon. News has reached me about the tragic affair with the antique dealer. I feel somehow responsible.'

Monsieur Pamplemousse found himself wondering how the Director had heard. Although he had skimmed through the rest of the Paris *journaux* he hadn't seen a mention of the murder in any of them.

'It seems as though our rendezvous wasn't meant, *Monsieur*.'

'It is a pity you didn't manage to get there before it happened,' said the Director. 'Never mind, it isn't the end of the world.'

It was for the antique dealer, thought Monsieur Pamplemousse grimly. He wondered if Monsieur Leclercq knew about the change in plans. 'In any case, I have since tried the address in Nice you gave me, and the shutters are down.'

'They are?' the Director sounded uneasy. 'I think, if I were you, Aristide, I would let matters rest there. There is no sense in putting your own life at risk. That is really why I was phoning you. It would be a terrible thing if you were to lose your appendages. Where would we be without them?'

Monsieur Pamplemousse stared at the receiver. There were times when Monsieur Leclercq's self-centredness quite took his breath away. He decided to change the subject.

'Since you mention telephones, *Monsieur*,' he said, 'I wonder if you could ask Veronique to send me some P37B forms. I am completely out of them.' The Director, his mind suddenly divorced from what had clearly been uppermost in it, emitted a clucking noise. 'Did I hear the word "some", Pamplemousse?'

'*Oui, Monsieur*. I shall need more than one. First of all I have had trouble with my lap-top...'

'This is very disappointing,' said the Director. 'I always thought you had a mechanical bent. That is why I selected you for the task of evaluating the new equipment. I normally set great store on your opinion in such matters...'

'Things are far from normal on the Côte d'Azur, *Monsieur*.'

'Have you tried seeking local assistance?'

'*Oui, Monsieur*. That was the start of my troubles.

'Using my new mobile, I first of all dialled the number pencilled on a sheet of paper. A Japanese/American voice with Irish overtones answered. Although it is often hard to tell, it was, I believe, electronically simulated and so incapable of holding a conversation. Either that or the person was in an extremely bad mood. Having informed me that I could make use of my handset, I was given a series of numbers and combinations of numbers I could press relating to various services, none of which, as it happened, bore any relation to the one I required…'

'Which was?'

'The name of the nearest dealer.'

'And?'

'I was put on standby to join the queue of those awaiting the next available advisor. I then went through a long sequence of listening to out-of-copyright music played on an electronic synthesiser, interspersed with announcements as to my place in the queue. As I recall, to begin with I was number 135. Finally, when I received the attention of a real live operator she put me through to the appropriate department where another electronic voice invited me to leave a message on the voicemail, having first pressed the star button followed by the extension number I required.

'However, since I had no idea what that was, I had to begin all over again. When I was eventually connected to the correct number another electronic voice informed me the office was closed for the next three days. It didn't offer any explanation as to why that was so.'

'What happened then?'

'I threw my mobile out of the hotel window, *Monsieur*. Which is why I require another P37B.'

During the long silence that followed, Monsieur Pamplemousse thought he detected a background noise which could only be described as a combination of heavy breathing and drumming.

'It sounds to me, Pamplemousse,' said the Director at long last, 'very much as though you are in urgent need of counselling. I will seek Matron's advice.'

'I would sooner have a new telephone,' said Monsieur Pamplemousse.

'You have only yourself to blame,' said Monsieur Leclercq. 'I agree that it was a Kafka-like experience, but would Kafka have so lost his temper as to throw his mobile over a *balcon*? A *balcon*, moreover, which, as I understand it from Veronique, who made the reservation, is several floors above sea level.'

'From all I have read of the author's life, *Monsieur*, particularly the period when he was in the employ of the Worker's Accident Insurance Institute of Prague, I doubt if he ever enjoyed the luxury of even so much as a Government surplus field telephone.

'But had he been through what I had been through, he would, I am sure, have made capital out of the experience. It would have provided him with more than sufficient material for yet another of his doom-laden tales.'

'This places me in a somewhat embarrassing situation, Pamplemousse. As you know, in response to numerous requests I have been busily upgrading our present equipment as part of my *Technologie Accomplissement* programme, but from the way things are going if we are not careful the whole thing may end up as a case of *sable mouvant*. What our friends across the ocean call "quicksanding".'

'The Americans have a succinct expression for most things,' said Monsieur Pamplemousse. '*Monsieur* has visited *les Etats-Unis* recently?'

It wouldn't surprise him. The Director often took it into his head to cross the Atlantic Ocean, and when he did he invariably returned armed with the latest jargon.

There was a pause. 'No, Aristide, it is an expression I came across when Chantal and I were staying with an uncle of hers in Corsica.'

Monsieur Pamplemousse stiffened. 'Not the one with Mafia connections?'

The Director suddenly changed gear. 'As you well know, Pamplemousse, through no fault of her own, my wife has Italian blood in her veins. It stems from her mother's side of the family. She has numerous uncles...'

'But we *are* talking about her Uncle Caputo,' persisted Monsieur Pamplemousse. 'The one whose nubile young daughter, Caterina, I had the misfortune to mislay when I was escorting her from Rome to Paris on the *Palentino* express?'

'Chantal's Uncle Caputo is Sicilian,' said the Director patiently. 'He has strict views on such matters. It just so happens he was in Corsica at the same time as we were. He was visiting the island in an advisory capacity; taking stock as it were with a view to creating critical mass in other parts of the world.'

'On the Côte d'Azur, *par exemple, Monsieur*?'

'No man is an island, Pamplemousse.'

'By the same token, *Monsieur*, no island is one man.'

'I would not wish to argue the point with Chantal's Uncle Caputo. He has his fingers in many pies and those pies are not exclusive to the land of his birth. He has a generous nature and over the years he has spread his favours far and wide. New York, San Marino, South America… He now has many families within a family; and it is their interests he is anxious to protect. He wished to be remembered to you, by the way. He said "he owes you one", whatever that may mean.

'It was through his connections with the electronic industry that I obtained the new equipment; on very favourable terms I may add. He assured me they were all factory fresh.'

'Doubtless they had fallen off the back of a lorry on their way to a dealer that very morning,' said Monsieur Pamplemousse, bitterly. 'It is one way of taking stock. Or perhaps it ran into an ambush. Did you not enquire into their origin at the time, *Monsieur*?'

'No, Pamplemousse, I did not. One does not ask too many questions of people like Uncle Caputo. Their patience is apt to wear thin. Remember, they adhere to a strict culture which involves *omèrta* or *acqua in bocca*: the code of silence. These things are not up for discussion.'

'I hope you are not planning to stay with him over Christmas,' said Monsieur Pamplemousse coldly.

'Why do you say that, Pamplemousse?'

'Because, *Monsieur*, if his family all sit round the table at meal times observing the code of silence, it will be a very sombre affair.'

Somewhat bruised by the encounter, Monsieur Pamplemousse returned to the table wondering if he had been over-precipitate in hanging up. If pressed, he would have to pretend they had been cut off.

He was just in time to attend the serving of the main course. As he took his seat the already plated dishes arrived. A group of four waiters materialised round the table and domes were lifted in unison.

The senior of the four remained to explain what they were about to eat. '*Poulet à la Niçoise*: chicken cooked with onion, tomato, olives and white wine. With it we serve *épinards aux pignons* and *fenouil braisé*: the spinach is cooked with pine nuts and orange blossom water. *Bon appetit*.'

'Yums!' said Mrs. Pickering as the waiter disappeared.

Monsieur Pamplemousse looked at her curiously. He assumed it was a compliment, but as with her husband it was often hard to read her mind.

This time, the dish was accompanied by a red wine from Bellet: Domaine Tempier. Aged in oak, it was served chilled in the manner of a young Beaujolais.

Mr. Pickering thought he detected a bouquet of cherries.

'They plant fruit trees amongst the vines, *Monsieur*,' explained Anouchka, returning the bottle to the ice bucket. 'It is well thought of.'

Monsieur Pamplemousse held up a chicken leg and examined it carefully. Again, there was not a trace of fat, indicating that the bird really had been allowed free range in the truest sense of the word, not just given a token square metre of earth to peck around in. The fennel had been lightly browned before being braised in stock from the chicken, giving it an almost translucent texture. It was pure Escoffier.

He raised his glass in a toast to the great man's memory.

'We have a lot to thank him for,' agreed Mr. Pickering. 'In

many ways he was the Leonardo da Vinci of the culinary world. If he'd been able to take out a patent on his *Pêche Melba* he could have lived on the royalties for the rest of his life. Since he introduced the frying pan to England we've never looked back. *And* he wasn't above inventing tinned tomatoes.'

Monsieur Pamplemousse picked up his knife and fork and was in the act of spearing a morsel of chicken breast when he notice the Maître d' hovering anxiously nearby as though expecting him to say something.

' *Superbe!*' he said. 'My compliments to the chef.'

'*Merci, Monsieur.*' The man executed a deep bow and in so doing contrived to bring his lips closer to Monsieur Pamplemousse's left ear.

'*Monsieur,*' he whispered, 'we have a very strict rule in the hotel about the use of mobile telephones during meal times.'

'Thank you for telling me,' said Monsieur Pamplemousse. 'I am delighted to hear it.' He made a mental note to inform the Director as soon as possible. 'I trust that many more hotels will follow your good example.'

The Maître d' looked relieved. 'I am pleased that you are pleased, *Monsieur.*'

'Good,' said Monsieur Pamplemousse. 'Now that we are all pleased, perhaps I can enjoy my meal in peace and quiet.'

'I will make sure your plate is kept warm for you while you are gone, *Monsieur.*'

Monsieur Pamplemousse stared at him. 'But I am not going anywhere...'

The Maître d' permitted himself a discrete cough. 'It seems the young *Monsieur* has been receiving calls,' he said. 'The telephone in his *gonflable* has been ringing constantly for the last half hour.'

A portion of chicken fell from Monsieur Pamplemousse's fork and landed on the floor. It disappeared in a flash.

'A telephone!' he exclaimed. 'In Pommes Frites' inflatable kennel?'

'*Oui, Monsieur.*'

'*Impossible!*'

'I am afraid not, *Monsieur*. There have been a number of complaints.' Reaching for a dome he placed a hand firmly on the back of Monsieur Pamplemousse's chair. 'If *Monsieur* would be so kind…'

'Not more bad news I trust?' said Mr. Pickering.

'It never rains,' said Monsieur Pamplemousse, 'but what it pours.'

'Especially when you are on the Riviera, Aristide,' said Doucette pointedly.

Monsieur Pamplemousse ignored the remark. 'Please carry on everyone. I have no idea how long I shall be.'

Having heard certain key words being mentioned following the unexpected windfall of a piece of chicken, Pommes Frites rose to his feet and padded after his master. Halfway down the steps leading to the beach he pricked up his ears. There was an insistent, albeit familiar ringing noise coming from his kennel, which he certainly hadn't noticed before. Quickening his pace, he pushed past Monsieur Pamplemousse and hastened towards the source.

Seconds later the ringing ceased and he emerged triumphant from his quarters holding the offending article firmly in his mouth.

Aware of the interest being shown by the sprinkling of late diners taking their *aperitifs* by the water before going up to the terrace, Monsieur Pamplemousse received the gift gratefully, wiped it dry with his handkerchief, and moved further along the beach out of hearing.

Holding the mobile to his ear his worst fears were realised.

'Pamplemousse! What *is* going on?'

'It is my mobile, *Monsieur*…'

'I know it is your mobile!' barked Monsieur Leclercq. 'Trigaux tells me it has been working for the past half hour. He has been trying to contact you.'

Monsieur Pamplemousse carefully detached a piece of

dried seaweed from the earpiece. 'Pommes Frites has only just located it, *Monsieur*. You will be pleased to know that apart from some tooth-marks it seems little the worse for wear. I may not have need of as many P37B's after all.'

'This is good news, Pamplemousse. We must be thankful for small mercies. Please give him my congratulations. I have said it before and I will say it again. Pommes Frites is an example to us all.

'However,' continued Monsieur Leclercq, 'that is not why I wish to speak to you. I have in front of me the results of your photographic expedition.'

'Aah!' Monsieur Pamplemousse brightened.

'You may indeed say "aah", Pamplemousse. Words fail me..'

'I am glad you are pleased with them, *Monsieur*.'

'Pleased!' thundered the Director. 'I am far from pleased! This is the *Folies* all over again. The *Folies* multiplied a hundred fold. It is no wonder you were dismissed from the *Sûreté*.'

'With respect, *Monsieur*, I wasn't dismissed. It was simply suggested that I should accept early retirement. Besides, it cannot be one hundred fold. The school is relatively small.'

'Please don't split hairs,' said Monsieur Leclercq wearily. 'Quite frankly, I am appalled. Whatever possessed you to take such pictures?'

'*Monsieur* does not like them? You do not think it will boost the circulation of the Staff Magazine should you decide to go public?'

'Given the way the poor girls are exposed to the elements,' said the Director severely, 'the only circulation that will need boosting is their own.'

'I have it on good authority, *Monsieur*, that they were adopting what is known as the preferred position during a thunderstorm.'

'I do not doubt that for one moment, Pamplemousse,' barked the Director. 'I also have no doubt that it is the preferred position for many other activities too numerous and unsavoury to mention. The only thing to be said for having one of your pictures on the front cover is that it would ensure a steady sale in some of the seedier establishments on the lower slopes of Montmartre. The whole thing is all the more unfortunate as I was about to prepare a Keynote Speech to all staff. I was hoping to illustrate it with some suitable blow-ups.'

Monsieur Pamplemousse gazed crestfallenly at the telephone as his dreams of having his name coupled with Cartier-Bresson or Doisneau began to fade.

'You mentioned Trigaux, *Monsieur*. Does he feel the same way?'

'I have no idea,' said the Director. 'As usual he was more concerned with technicalities than subject matter; variations in photographic rather than bodily exposure. Some of the most prolonged flashes of lightning caused a certain amount of confusion in the automatic system. However, in his report he has pointed out that in the latter half of the film, presumably after you had stopped to change position, there is one *derrière* missing.'

'*Pardon, Monsieur*? There must be some mistake. A trick of the light.'

'No, Pamplemousse. There is no mistake. I know because I have been over the enlargements very carefully myself; not once, but several times. In the first set of pictures there are forty-eight *derrières* of various shapes and sizes. In the second there are only forty-seven. It is all the more apparent because the missing one belonged to a pupil who is – or shall we say, *was – très solide*. Also, in the beginning of the sequence she was the only one looking straight at the lens.'

'Was she the third one from the right in the last row?'

'How do you know that, Pamplemousse?' barked the Director suspiciously.

'If it is who I think it is, *Monsieur*, I know where she was standing.'

'No doubt there is a simple explanation,' said the Director.

'No doubt, *Monsieur*.'

Simple, perhaps, but in what respect? If it was the Russian girl, she certainly hadn't been with her parents at dinner. Perhaps that accounted for their worried looks. If she had gone missing, he hoped the school had a stand-in for tonight's performance.

'*Monsieur*,' he began. 'In case you wish to contact me again, you may like to know that the use of mobile telephones at meal times is *interdit*. I have been giving the matter some thought. We shall need a new symbol, of course, and I wonder if perhaps a telephone receiver beneath crossed knives and forks would be suitable?'

'*Monsieur*...'

Removing the receiver from his ear, Monsieur Pamplemousse looked at the display panel and was just in time to see a flashing battery symbol before it faded from view.

'*Merde!*'

Ever alive to his master's moods, Pommes Frites disappeared into his kennel. He had been keeping careful watch on Monsieur Pamplemousse's changing facial expressions while he had been talking; the occasional raising of his eyes towards the heavens, the staring at the object in his hand as though he couldn't believe his eyes. Now the utterance of yet another key word; in fact not just the word itself, but the way in which it had been said, clinched matters for him.

Clearly, his first present had not achieved the one hundred per cent success rate he had hoped for. That being so it was time to have another go. Hidden under a blanket at the back of his kennel, he had a selection of items culled since his arrival: sticks, bits of seaweed, the remains of an old beach ball, a handkerchief covered in blood, several sea shells which had taken his fancy...

Pommes Frites spent some time sorting through the pile until he found what he was looking for. This time, as he presented it to his master, he knew that he had struck gold in more ways than one. The fact that he was wearing his "there's plenty more where that came from" expression passed unnoticed.

Returning to the table, Monsieur Pamplemousse waved aside his chicken. Suddenly he had no stomach for it. His mind was too full of other things. He looked around the crowded terrace. The Russians were no longer there.

'I take back what I said earlier,' said Mr. Pickering. 'About your work, I mean. Is it always like this?'

Monsieur Pamplemousse shrugged. 'We all think the grass is greener on the other side of the fence, but more often than not it is an illusion.'

Mr. Pickering eyed him thoughtfully, then abruptly changed the subject. 'For the benefit of your records,' he said, 'I have been making notes and I have come to the conclusion that for a country which produced Pasteur, its inhabitants spend a great deal of their time searching out unpasteurised cheese.

'There is a Banon, of course – a Banon à la Feuille made from goat's milk, a Chèvre Fermier du Château-Vert made by a farmer on Mont Ventoux, and what the waiter referred to as his *pièce de résistance,* a Brebis de Tende made from ewe's milk.

'According to him the only place you'll find it is in Nice. In the Cours Saleya market – and then only if you are lucky! He also presented us each with a glass of *rosé*, compliments of the house. I think he was frightened we might spoil the flavour if we stuck with the red.'

Conscious of Pommes Frites' find weighing heavily in his trouser pocket, Monsieur Pamplemousse listened with only half an ear. He didn't know whether to tell the others or not, but in the end decided against it. Instead, he opted for a breakfast meeting with Mr. Pickering and Todd in the morning.

Doucette came to his rescue by suggesting she and Mrs. Pickering pay a visit to some botanical gardens nearby: the

Jardin Thuret. 'Over three thousand tropical trees and plants and it's free!'

'Say no more,' said Mrs. Pickering. 'It appeals to my Scots blood.'

'Another popular misconception,' said Mr. Pickering. 'Scottish people are far from mean, they just happen to be canny and warm with it. That's one of the reasons why I married Jan.'

The dessert – *Glace à la fleur d'Oranger* – an unbelievably light ice cream flavoured with orange blossom water and decorated with chocolate shavings – came and went. But for once Monsieur Pamplemousse would have been hard put to describe it. He was anxious to bring the meal to an end.

'Why did you marry me, Aristide?' Doucette posed the question when they were back in their room.

'Because I pictured all the wonderful holidays we wouldn't spend together, Couscous,' said Monsieur Pamplemousse, reaching in his trouser pocket. 'And because I value your opinion on matters such as this.'

Doucette took the object from him, held it up to the light, then weighed it in her hand. 'It looks very valuable,' she said. 'It feels valuable too. Where ever did you get it?'

'I didn't. Pommes Frites found it.'

'You don't think...'

'That it is what we were supposed to collect? I'm afraid I do.'

'Have you told Monsieur Leclercq?'

Monsieur Pamplemousse shook his head. 'I have already had two long conversations on the telephone with him this evening. That is enough for any man.'

'But I expected it to be a painting of some kind.'

'He didn't say what it was. In fact, I'm beginning to suspect he didn't even know.'

It was meant to be a surprise for his wife. Where Pommes Frites found it is another matter. But it must have been somewhere quite near here. As for *when*, perhaps even on the night we arrived. It is possible there was a struggle and during the course of it our man managed to throw it away.'

Doucette weighed the object again. 'But that would mean it was before he...'

'...before he was dismembered.' Monsieur Pamplemousse completed the sentence for her. 'I said you have the makings of a good detective, Couscous. You would have passed the exam with flying colours.'

'I'm not so sure.' Doucette gave another shiver. 'I think I may have asked to be excused my practicals.'

As they began getting ready for bed, she crossed to the wardrobe. 'Has it occurred to you to wonder why Monsieur Leclercq picked on us to carry out his mission?'

'Sometimes, Couscous,' said Monsieur Pamplemousse, 'it is better not to pose such questions. But I am beginning to suspect the worst.'

As Doucette opened the wardrobe door she stifled any reply she might have had. 'Aristide! What have you done?'

'It is what is known in the trade as impulse buying,' said Monsieur Pamplemousse. He watched Doucette's reflection in the mirror as she held the beach dress against herself.

'But when did you put it here?'

'It must have happened when I rang the Director back,' said Monsieur Pamplemousse innocently.

'It is exactly the right size. How did you guess?'

'I didn't. I looked at the label in the old one before I went out yesterday morning.'

'Once a detective always a detective.'

Monsieur Pamplemousse sighed. Even Doucette was doing it now. It was a case of variations on a theme. Perhaps it was true and there was no escape.

'It is also,' he said, 'because absence makes the heart grow fonder and I was thinking while I was on my way to Nice, I really don't know what I would do without you.'

'Sometimes, Aristide,' said Doucette, 'you say the nicest things.'

Did he fall or was he pushed?

Todd and Mr. Pickering were already seated at a corner table on the terrace when Monsieur Pamplemousse and Pommes Frites arrived for breakfast. Mr. Pickering, umbrella hooked over the back of his chair, was studying what appeared to be a very old Baedeker guide to Southern France. Todd was doodling on a lined yellow legal pad.

Mr. Pickering looked up enquiringly. *'Ca va?'*

Monsieur Pamplemousse responded with a non-committal up and down wave of his right hand. He couldn't speak for Pommes Frites, but after the episode at the school he had woken during the night feeling somewhat less than 100%. He felt as though rain had seeped into every joint in his body.

'Even the computer didn't recognise my voice this morning,' he croaked. 'The spell-check has been having a field day. Everything was underlined in red. It will need reprogramming.'

'Join the morning-after club,' said Todd. 'I'm still feeling impaired from last night.' He gave Monsieur Pamplemousse a quizzical look. 'From all I hear, it sounds like you got more equipment than the CIA. Right?'

'I know a little restaurant down by the port in Antibes,' said Mr. Pickering, tactfully changing the subject, 'where the fish soup is recommended by ear, nose and throat specialists everywhere. It's a case of kill or cure. Either it will bring your voice back or else it will silence it forever. As an added plus the garlic not only kills bacteria and viruses, it stimulates the appetite.

'In the meantime, to quote Macaulay, "An invitation to breakfast is a proof that one is held to be good company."'

'Not in the US it ain't,' said Todd. 'Meaning no offence to the present assembly. Know what I mean?'

'Anyway, that was in the nineteenth century,' said Mr. Pickering mildly. 'Before the advent of power breakfasts.

'Todd is having trouble with his order,' he added.

'I told the waitron I wanted my eggs sunny side up and you know what he said? "Monsieur, on ze Côte d'Azur *everything* is sunny side up." Cheeky son of a bitch! As for hash browns, nobody outside the States seems to have heard of them.'

'You can always rate a hotel by the quality of the breakfast,' said Monsieur Pamplemousse. 'If the butter comes in a dish rather than a packet, if the *confiture* is home-made and not in a tiny pot, and if the milk is fresh and not Long Life, you can't go far wrong.'

'Even so,' said Mr. Pickering, 'getting what you want can still be a complicated business. The Swedes are apt to start their day with pickled herring and soured milk. In the Netherlands it's cheese and sliced meats. In the Balkans you are quite likely to end up with soup. Scotland has its porridge; Asia its rice. If you order bacon and egg in England, that's exactly what you get – one egg; a throwback to a war that ended nearly sixty years ago. In America they take it for granted you mean two, but you practically have to fill in a questionnaire as to how you want them cooked. And when they arrive you find fruit you hadn't asked for served on the side. Toast is even worse. Is to be white bread? Rye? Wholemeal? Sourdough? Pumpernickel? Boston brown? . . . the list of possibilities is endless.'

'Don't forget Mexico,' said Todd. 'Know what a Mexican breakfast is? A cigarette and a cup of coffee.'

'Monet had the right idea,' continued Mr. Pickering. 'He used to combine the whole lot; a good English fry-up – Dutch cheese – sausages – toast and marmalade – and since he couldn't abide staying up late because it upset his routine, he had any guests round to eat with him then rather than at dinner time.'

Monsieur Pamplemousse cast an eye over the other tables. 'How about *Les Ivans*?'

'Those hairballs?' said Todd. 'I doubt if they'll be around this morning if that's what you're thinking. Rumour has it their kid – the one with the Cruella de Vil smile – is missing, believed stolen. Although who'd want it, search me? When the time comes for her to get married, her Hope Chest is going to look pretty sorry for itself. Right?'

'I wouldn't be too sure,' said Monsieur Pamplemousse, remembering the school concert. 'It could end up very well lined.'

'Perhaps she's "resting",' said Mr. Pickering. 'Show-biz may be getting her down. She didn't strike me as being an over-scheduled child.'

'*Mais* . . . ' Monsieur Pamplemousse was about to tell them the news concerning his photographs when the waiter arrived with Todd's breakfast.

He used the opportunity to show his room key. 'In France,' he said, picking up the conversation where it had been left off, 'we simply say *"un petit déjeuner complet, s'il vous plaît."*'

'*Café, Monsieur?*' asked the waiter. '*Jus d'orange?*'

'I told you it wasn't easy,' murmured Mr. Pickering.

'Make it for two,' said Monsieur Pamplemousse. 'But no *café* or *jus d'orange* with the second. Just a bowl of fresh water.'

'*Oui, Monsieur.*'

'The thing I like about French waiters,' said Mr. Pickering, 'is that nothing throws them.'

'Talking of eggs...' Monsieur Pamplemousse felt inside a trouser pocket and found what he was looking for. It was resting in a tiny pile of dried sand. 'What do you make of this?' Removing an ovoid object, he laid it on the table.

Todd gave a whistle under his breath. 'Fabergé, no less.'

'How did you come by it?' asked Mr. Pickering.

'Pommes Frites gave it to me.'

'I always knew he was dog of taste and discernment.'

Hearing his name mentioned, Pommes Frites poked his head out from under the tablecloth, looked around, sniffed, then withdrew to await the arrival of the food.

'I suspect,' said Monsieur Pamplemousse, 'it had more to do with the torso that was washed up the other night. Would you say it is genuine?'

Mr. Pickering picked up the egg, blew away a few grains of sand still clinging to the gold filigree decoration of its white enamelled shell, and held it up to the light. 'I'm no great expert...

'I know that Peter Carl Fabergé was born in the middle of the nineteenth century. He wasn't a craftsman himself, but he was a brilliant designer and he had the wit and the foresight to realise that a block of gold can be fashioned into something infinitely more valuable. To that end, when he took over the family business he gathered together some of the most gifted craftsmen in Europe and set them to work.

'As I understand it, the two foremost work-masters – Michael Evlampievitch Perchin – a Russian, and a Scandinavian called Henrik Wigstrom, used to stamp their initials on everything they did. I know that any new piece on the market should be treated with a certain amount of reserve, but it's one way of checking the authenticity.'

He turned the egg over and took a closer look. 'Apart from that, there are usually Russian assay marks showing the purity of the metal, which was measured in *zolotnics* – roughly four *zolotnics* to one U.K. carat; so 18 carots would be 72 *zolotnics*. Pure silver was even higher. Something like this, which has a lot of decoration, probably used a lower grade of metal as the enamelling adheres to it better, but that doesn't necessarily make it any less valuable, given all the gold motifs and trelliswork, not to mention diamonds and rubies. As for the place of origin, in the old days each city had it's own mark.' He flipped open the hinged cover. 'My guess is that it was meant for holding pills.'

'I'll tell you something for free,' said Todd, not to be outdone. 'I wouldn't go flashing it around. Why? Because it ain't healthy. Right?' He took the egg from Mr. Pickering, and like Doucette before him, weighed it carefully in his hand first, as though about to play a game of boules, then fished in a pocket and produced a magnifying glass.

'It's got Henrik Wigstrom's stamp all right. But there's a national mark, rather than a regional one – a woman in a traditional head-dress – which makes it after 1896.'

'How much is it worth?' He shrugged. 'How do you put a value on any work of art? As much as the market will stand, I guess. If it's for real, this kind of thing is irreplaceable. Malcolm Forbes would know. He's the multi-millionaire guy who runs Forbes financial magazine. At the last count he'd gotten himself almost as many as there are in the whole of the Soviet Union.'

'Very tiny unadorned eggs currently fetch £4,000 - £5,000 in Switzerland,' said Mr. Pickering. 'At the other end of the scale, a few years ago what was known as the Imperial Winter Egg was sold for just under £4,000,000.'

'If it is possible to forge a complex miniature work of art like this,' said Monsieur Pamplemousse, retrieving it, 'then surely it is possible to forge the signatures?'

'Bingo!' said Todd. 'Hole in one! It's one of the scams the Russian Mafiya run. That's how I got to know a bit about it. The story goes they've taken over a jewellery factory in Budapest specialising in the restoration of antiques – and that includes Fabergé eggs. The chances of an owner getting the original one back is something I wouldn't like to take a bet on. It's more likely to end up on the International market.'

'Imitation is not only the sincerest form of flattery,' broke in Mr. Pickering, 'it's often the most lucrative, particularly if the original artist is dead.'

'If all the Renoirs in Hollywood were laid end to end,' said Todd, 'it would be a hell of a long walk. Right? Vanity is on the forger's side. No one likes to admit they've been taken for a ride – especially when their judgement is called into question.'

'I've always understood that if you put a fake Fabergé alongside the real thing you don't need to be all that much of an expert to tell the two apart,' said Mr. Pickering. 'It's a matter of attention to detail and the quality of the workmanship. The enamelling in a genuine egg has a translucency which only comes from the technique of using many layers. If there is any kind of wallpapering effect – a rippling – rather like the pattern left in the wet sand after the tide has gone out – then it will have been applied to one of the inner layers rather than on the surface.

'If its original box were available that would be the best clue. The quality of the workmanship in those was superb too.'

'Unless Pommes Frites has it,' said Monsieur Pamplemousse, 'I'm afraid that is how it came.'

'Like I say,' broke in Todd, 'if the Ruskies are involved, watch your step.'

'The thing is,' Mr. Pickering lowered his voice, 'As you've probably guessed by now, I'm here on what you might call a working holiday. Mrs. Pickering doesn't really approve of my mixing business with pleasure, but the powers that be have decreed otherwise. How about you?'

'I am what *les journaux* usually refer to as an innocent bystander,' said Monsieur Pamplemousse. 'And that is the truth. I rarely mix business and pleasure with Madame Pamplemousse either.'

'And I got no plans for going plural,' said Todd.

Seeing the waiter about to arrive with the *petit dejeuner*, Monsieur Pamplemousse slipped the egg back into his pocket, and moved his chair slightly so that there was room for Pommes Frites' water bowl.

'You can tell me to mind my own beeswax if you'd rather not open up,' said Todd, when they were alone again. 'On the other hand . . .'

Taking Todd to mean what he thought he meant, Monsieur Pamplemousse

brought the other two up to date, omitting nothing apart from giving an edited version of his last conversation with the Director. He wasn't sure how news of Uncle Caputo's involvement would go down with Todd.

At the end of his story they sat in silence for a moment or two.

Mr. Pickering was the first to speak. 'You think the egg may be the "work of art" you were supposed to collect?'

'It is the most likely explanation,' said Monsieur Pamplemousse. 'I can't think of another.'

'And for some reason our disarticulated friend who was supposed to deliver it fell foul of the Russian Mafiya on the way?'

'I fear so.'

'So how did your dog come by it?' asked Todd.

'I think something must have happened while my wife and I were at the school concert. In retrospect, when we came out he was very restless, and clearly from the way he behaved when what remained of the body was washed up, he evidently made some kind of connection in his mind.'

'Criminal gangs everywhere have a vested interest in instability,' said Todd thoughtfully, 'but it's a question of territories. You know what I mean?'

'What about the Beaune Summit that happened a few years ago,' broke in Monsieur Pamplemousse. 'The Heads of all the crime rings in the world are supposed to have met up and worked out a pact parcelling up the territories?'

'When it comes to territory, no one wants to give up what they've already staked a claim to. That goes for the guy who gets shoved off his patch at a baseball game, or finds someone parked on his front drive when he gets back home, all the way up through Northern Ireland via Bosnia, to the Arabs and the Jews slugging it out in the Middle East. I'll give you a dollar for every North America Indian you can show me who doesn't still harbour a grudge.

'There's what you might call a certain amount of unrest amongst the natives over here. The French and Italian Mafia don't take kindly to strangers muscling in. Maybe this was a warning shot on the part of the Ruskies, making the point that they want a part of the action. Right?'

'Which is?'

'In this part of the world? Mostly drugs – although historically in France that's Marseilles territory. Prostitution. Door to door Insurance...'

'The protection racket.' added Mr. Pickering, by way of translation.

'Applied statistics...'

'Another word for gambling,' broke in Mr. Pickering. 'Carried out by "members of a career-offender cartel".' He gave a sigh. 'And they used to say the French have a phrase for it!'

Todd snorted. 'Meaning no disrespect to our friend here. We're in a country where they call female Traffic Wardens goddam "Periwinkles"!'

'Not officially,' said Monsieur Pamplemousse. 'Officially the *Conseil Supérior de la Langue*, who are responsible for these things, have more important matters on their mind – such as whether or not we should do away with the circumflex accent.'

'Anyway,' said Todd, 'back home it's a way of brushing problems under the carpet. Like we don't have people being made redundant any more. They suffer an "involuntary career event" and get "uninstalled." People don't die in hospital; they endure "terminal living" leading to "negative patient care outcome". It all comes down to the same thing in the end.'

'So what is so different about the Russian Mafia?' asked Monsieur Pamplemousse.

'What's different about the Mafiya? I'll tell you what it ain't for a start. It ain't anything like the Mafia as we used to know it. Right? The old-style Cosa Nostra was "family" in all senses of the word. It had its Godfathers and its hierarchy, but at least you knew where you stood. You knew each family's territory, and they knew that you knew.

'Jimmy "Jerome" Squillante had the New York garbage all sewn up until his car was put through a crusher and turned into a cube with him inside it. The Anastasio brothers looked after the waterfront. The Gambino family got a percentage of every load of mixed concrete in the Manhattan construction industry until they had to share it with three other families; the Genovese, the Colombos and the Luccheses.

'Pinning it on them was something else again. In the end it was the I.R.S. – the Inland Revenue Service – who got them for non-payment of taxes. Once the I.R.S. latch on to something they never give up.

'Don't get me wrong. I'm not doing a whitewash job. I'm simply saying they're predictable. You know where you stand. Right?

'*Everything* is different about the Russian Mafiya. They got no rules; no disciplines. They're like a bunch of unguided missiles. In the beginning they used to arrive in a country with a suitcase full of cash and a thousand of ways of getting rid of it. Paying for everything on the spot: goods, services, the man who comes to do the garden.

'The worst thing that happened to the Western world was when Russia lifted the Iron Curtain. Everyone wanted it to happen, but nobody had given any thought to the flip side of the coin.

'They didn't reckon on U.S. aid money going straight into banks owned and run by the Mafiya. Wholesale robbery of their homeland took place during Peristroika.

'The government emptied their gaols of all the worst offenders and encouraged them to leave the country. Given the carrot, a lot of them looked around and saw that Israel has no extradition facilities in place, which made it a good bolt-hole, so they took blood samples and suddenly discovered they had Jewish ancestry. From there they moved on to other places; America first of all, then onward and outward.

'Go to Brighton Beach, U.S.A., and you could be in Odessa U.S.S.R. Instead of getting a few cents on every bag of cement shifted in New York, like the old style Mafia, they moved into oil. In the space of five years, bootlegging gasolene in the East Coast area was netting them a cool $8 billion dollars a year plus.

'How did they get away with it? In one word – bureaucracy. There's nothing like creating a lot of phoney paperwork to slow things up. They've gotten the best shysters in the business to set up strings of small companies that can go bankrupt overnight if need be. It's what's called daisy-chaining.'

'Somehow I can't see our own Brighton beach suffering the same fate,' said Mr. Pickering. 'The landladies wouldn't stand for it. They have strict rules.'

Monsieur Pamplemousse thought of the cargo ship he'd seen loading up with cement in Nice and wondered. It had been bound for Amsterdam. A consignment of drugs mixed in would probably never be found. It would be like looking for the proverbial needle in a haystack.

'It could happen over here,' said Todd, reading his thoughts. 'How many French cops speak Russian? That gives them an edge to start with.'

'And you think our friend is dipping his toes in the water...'

'He's no Dudley Doorite, that's for sure. And he ain't here to enjoy the sunshine. These boys don't goof around. Right?

'The ones that have already made the trip now have their *dachas* in the hills behind Cannes. The newcomers think nothing of renting a yacht with a full crew for $5,000 a day – cash down. Doors get held open for them.'

'You are absolutely correct.' Mr.Pickering grew serious for a moment. 'People in glass houses shouldn't throw stones. Money-laundering has become big business. At the last count the IMF estimate was that it runs to between $600bn and $1,500bn per year. And it isn't just the criminal element. Big corporations do it, even governments get involved.'

'I'm surprised you make the distinction,' said Todd.

'Remember Oliver North and the Iranian scandal? Remember the BCCI scandal in the U.K.? The biggest money laundering operation ever; and all under the benevolent eye of the Bank of England. I doubt if we'll ever hear the truth of that one.'

'And nobody throws the book at them?'

'Listen,' said Todd. 'If you've spent time in a Russian Gulag nothing the West can throw at you is gonna hurt. The guys who run those places had their trade handed down from the time of the Revolution when hatred bred untold atrocities.

'Besides, crime has infiltrated all levels of Russian society. The country is full of people who want to get rich quick and they don't care how they do it. Guns are easy to come by. And not just guns. They have off-the-shelf helicopters, guided missiles, nuclear hardware – you name it.

'They've even been known to ship a submarine complete with a full crew to their friends in Colombia.'

'People smuggling is big business. It's the current growth industry and there's no shortage of applicants. Bosnians, Chinese, Afghans, Iraqis – all prepared to pay any price to buy their freedom; Moscow has become a major part of the pipeline.

'In some ways they are cruder than the old style Mafia; in others – like in electronics – they're more sophisticated. Mixed in with the old, there is a new breed of criminal, born in an electronic age. They have the advantage of instant communication in real time and they're into share dealing via the Internet in a big way. And I'm not talking straight dealing.

'As for money-laundering. Take a look in the Guinness Book of Records. Worldwide, the Mafiya have control of over 400 banks with a total annual profit of $250 billion. That gives them a hell of a lot of clout. We're not talking peanuts.'

Monsieur Pamplemousse made the mental leap from Nice harbour to the school and its array of aerials. At least the Almighty had made sure they now had one less.

'In real terms,' said Mr. Pickering, 'it means that a relatively tiny group of people have it in their power to destroy a small country if they feel like it.'

'And the bigger ones can do nothing about it?'

'From time to time they try. Getting them together is the hardest job.'

'I tell you something else,' said Todd. 'When you do get them all together what happens? Straight off you have an argument. Right?'

'It's as I was saying yesterday evening,' broke in Mr. Pickering. 'Different countries have different standards. Some lean over backwards to encourage the investment of money. They don't question where it comes from. The biggest mistake in the world is to assume we all see things in the same light or even have the same ground rules.'

'It begins the moment you are born,' agreed Monsieur Pamplemousse. 'Take the simple matter of twins. In your country the first one to be born is considered to have started life first and therefore is the elder of the two. In France the second to emerge is considered to be the elder because it was conceived first.'

'That's the kind of concept lawyers grow fat on back home,' said Todd.

'It's another way of looking at it,' said Mr. Pickering. 'Your Gertrude Stein summed it up when she said the French are logical and the English are rational.'

Monsieur Pamplemousse was suddenly reminded of the conversation he'd overheard in the train.

'I can give you a typical case in point. I have heard that breast feeding isn't allowed in your Houses of Parliament on the grounds that it is forbidden to bring refreshments into the chamber.'

'A non-sequitur if ever I heard one,' said Mr. Pickering. 'But it sounds authentic.'

'Bring in a rule like that in the U.S.,' said Todd, 'and the House of Representatives would be flooded with women baring their breasts as they bring their kids in for the morning break.'

'Perish the thought!' exclaimed Mr. Pickering.

'It's the way the cookie crumbles,' said Todd.

Mr. Pickering shrugged. 'I haven't heard that expression for years. It's good to know some things don't change.'

'The world doesn't change either,' said Todd, 'even if it does get a new coat of paint from time to time. Right?'

Monsieur Pamplemousse brushed away his *croissant* crumbs. 'In French schools,' he said quietly, 'children are taught that there are three alternatives for everything.'

'So what are you saying?' asked Todd.

'Either the Mafiya are left to get on with it, or it is a case of waiting until Governments get together, which could take forever. The third alternative could be that the local families have some ideas of their own.' He thought of the missing daughter. The truth was that in the short term when push came to shove he would be tempted to put his money on Uncle Caputo.

Mr. Pickering closed his guide book with a snap, jotted down an address on a scrap of paper, and handed it across the table.

'That is the name of the restaurant I mentioned. If you do go there, give my regards to the Madame. And if you fancy a stroll afterwards, take a look at the Fair down by the harbour. There, you will be able to see the Russian Mafiya at work.' Reaching for his pipe, he made play of looking for some matches, then seemed to think better of it.

'*À bientôt*. It's time for my daily dip.' With an absentminded wave he was gone.

'He's a nice guy,' said Todd when they were alone. 'But have you noticed something. He never lights that fire-stick of his. He even has it in his mouth when he goes in the sea. I reckon he's got some kind of electronic gear inside it.

'Another thing...there's something funny about that guide-book he carries around. Guess what date it was published? 1914! I asked him about it and you know what he said? "It *is* the 6th revised edition, old man!".'

Monsieur Pamplemousse wondered if Todd knew about the umbrella. 'There is no knowing with the British what they are up to,' he said. 'Tell me about Antibes harbour.'

'There's this travelling Fair. When it arrived for the summer season a few weeks ago it was run by Rumanians. Now the Mafiya get 50 per cent of the takings.'

'Just like that?' said Mr. Pamplemousse.

'Not just like that,' said Todd. 'I guess there would have been a little bit of leaning on the players beforehand. Talk of a torch job maybe. We'll never know. Old style Omerta doesn't just mean silence between members of the Mafia. It goes for the victims too. Threaten the lives of their families and they dry up like a clam. Accidents can happen – especially in a fairground. The body that was washed up the other night was either a warning or a statement – and not just to the antique trade.'

'Is it worth it?'

'You familiar with bunjee jumping?'

'I have seen pictures.'

'Wait until you see it for real, but in reverse. This is state of the art stuff. You can charge the earth for a go on the Human Slingshot Ride. People queue up to pay 150 francs to be strapped in an ejector seat and projected 150 feet into the air. For another 100 francs you get a take-home video showing what it's like to experience 3g of acceleration followed almost immediately by free fall.

'Like I say, it's bungee jumping in reverse, except you have two cords. Instead of acting as a brake, the elastic projects you upwards so the sky's the limit.'

'I can't wait,' said Monsieur Pamplemousse drily. He glanced down. 'I know someone who won't be going on it.'

He wouldn't receive any thanks if he let Pommes Frites loose on garlic soup. One member of the family would be deemed quite sufficient.

Their room was empty when he arrived upstairs. Doucette's tray had been collected, the bed made. He guessed she and Mrs. Pickering must have already left for their outing together.

Looking out of the window he saw Mr. Pickering enjoying a paddle. His trousers were rolled up to just below his knees and it was as Todd had said. He had his pipe firmly gripped between his clenched teeth. The business end was pointing towards the hotel. One of the penthouse suites on the top floor to judge by the angle.

The beach was beginning to fill up. A North African bearing a tray-load of assorted gifts threaded his way in and out of the recumbent bodies on his first excursion of the day. There were no takers.

With time to kill before lunch, Monsieur Pamplemousse suddenly felt at a loose end. Leaving the *Bâton de Berger* just inside Pommes Frites' kennel in case he got hungry (in the old days it had often signalled the end of a case, and the most effective way he knew of destroying evidence. Even the nuts were reprocessed beyond recognition) he set off to walk into Antibes.

Taking a short cut, he joined the main coast road near the Port de la Salis and followed it until he reached the old harbour in Antibes itself.

The restaurant turned out to be one of those places where the fare probably hadn't changed since the *Madame* running it had taken over from her Mother. Entering it was like taking a step back in time.

Ricard ashtrays and blue Pernod water jugs, each containing a small posy of flowers, were dotted around the room. The sun shining through net curtains made filigree patterns on the marble topped table as he sat down near the window and took stock of his surroundings: bent-wood chairs for those facing the wall, faded red plush banquettes for those facing outwards.

Just inside the door there was an old wooden hat-stand,

and alongside that a numbered rack, presumably where regulars kept their napkins. A well-worn path in the patterned tiled floor led to a zinc bar, behind which was an etched glass mirror. Beneath the mirror there was a shelf of inverted Paris goblets and a variety of *pastis* bottles.

Drawings of fishing boats adorned the dark wood-panelled walls. Among them, on the wall near the bar, was a framed embroidery bearing the words *L'aigo-boulido sauvo le vido*. Loosely translated he took it to mean "garlic soup saves lives". A bead curtain separated the main room from the kitchen, and behind it he could hear the business-like sound of a baguette slicer at work.

In the far corner an ancient radio did battle against noise coming from the fair, while from under a table an Alsatian dog kept watch on the comings and goings. It was another reason why he wasn't wholly sorry to have left Pommes Frites behind. The world had enough problems over territorial rights as it was.

The *Madame* appeared, negotiated the beads with practised ease, spread a brown paper "table cloth" in front of him, and having placed a single spoon on top, stood poised, order pad and pencil at the ready as she awaited his order. As if she didn't know!

A Ricard, a *L'aigo-boulido*, a *demi-pichet* of red *vin ordinaire*... each item received a nod of approval, followed by the ultimate accolade of *parfait*.

What more could anyone wish for? If they did they were welcome to go elsewhere!

A copy of his order was removed from the pad and placed under a jug. Moments later the *pastis* materialised, along with a jug of ice-cold water and a basket of bread.

The soup came as an individual portion served at the table. First to arrive was a generous helping of hot garlic *bouillon* containing a sprig of sage and a bayleaf. Sprinkled with olive oil and stirred, it was added a little at a time to a bowl containing beaten egg yolk. After the two had been combined and served, the remaining mixture was returned to a double boiler to keep warm.

The dish was all that Mr. Pickering had cracked it up to be. With every spoonful Monsieur Pamplemousse felt his voice returning. It cried out for a second helping.

Finally wiping the bowl clean with the last of the *baguette*, he drained his glass and called for *l'addition*. The *Madame* didn't seem at all surprised. On the contrary, the state of his bowl brought a smile of pleasure to her face.

'You must be looking forward to the Fair moving on.'

She gave a shrug. 'It brings in the evening trade.'

He wondered. They wouldn't be the choicest customers in town. It was hard to picture Mr. Pickering taking his evening meal there. And yet . . . passing on the other's message produced another warm smile. Clearly, he had left his mark.

Leaving the bistro, he headed towards the harbour. Worming his way through a cluster of tow trucks and mobile homes – mostly Ford, but with a sprinkling of other makes: Citroen T55, Renault, Opel and Berliet – the usual hodge-podge of fairground vehicles, he felt a renewed spring in his step.

The noise grew louder: a pot pourri of sound. Organ music from an old Bayol children's carousel with carved wooden gingerbread pigs; the steady crack of rifle shots from a shooting gallery – all mirrors and gilt and lined with portraits of film stars contemporary at the time when it was built – Maurice Chevalier, Charlie Chaplin, Fernandel. Girlish screams came from a wooden boat as it hurtled down a chute before landing with a huge splash in the water below. Above it all, there was the low roar of generators and the characteristic smell of discharging electricity from the dodgem cars. The big wheel was doing a roaring trade.

On past the maze with its distorting mirrors, and the "Boîte à Rire" Fun House; if the graphics in the style of Jacques Coutois outside were anything to go by it was another throwback to the days when travelling fairs provided prostitutes for their customers. He wondered if the Russians might revive the custom and whether they frequented the bistro where he'd just had lunch.

At the far end he came across the ride he was looking for. His first sight of it was when a steel cage-like object suddenly hurtled skywards, executed a quick flip, then disappeared again. He quickened his pace.

There were more people watching than there were queuing to have a go. Even so, there was clearly a brisk turnover. As he joined the crowd two girls paid their money and began screaming with excitement the moment they were strapped into the seats. There was a pause while the cables hanging from the two elevated steel support poles – one on each side – tightened and took up the strain, then the operator stood clear and pressed a foot pedal.

Paradoxically, as the cage was catapulted upwards the screaming stopped. It resumed as it reached the end of its run, rotated through 360 degrees, then bounced up and down four or five times before finally coming to rest. It was all over in less than a minute.

The operator lowered it gently to the ground before locating it onto a spigot protruding from the platform.

Monsieur Pamplemousse had a feeling he recognised the man, but perhaps it was simply that he looked like fairground operators the world over.

Feeling a presence at his side he turned and found himself face to face with the person he had come to think of as Krushev's minder. Close to his teeth looked even more metallic than they had from a distance. He wondered if he cleaned them with regularly with metal polish. If he didn't, did they ever go rusty during the night?

'Fancy a ride?' It wasn't so much a question as a statement.

'I have better things to do with my life than entrust it to a set of elastic bands,' said Monsieur Pamplemousse. 'Particularly after a good lunch.' He was about to move away when he felt something small, round and hard pressing into his back, propelling him forward.

'We need to talk.' The man spoke French with an American accent.

As they reached the head of the queue a couple who had been about to climb into the cage began to remonstrate.

There was a short sharp exchange of words. The girl stifled a cry of alarm, her companion went pale.

Monsieur Pamplemousse made a quick calculation of his options. There wasn't a uniform in sight, and for the moment at least no one in the waiting crowd looked as though they would be on his side; if anything it was very much the reverse.

He felt himself being forced into the nearest seat. 'Breathe out, *Monsieur*.' The operator bent over him.

Monsieur Pamplemousse turned his head away and obeyed. What sounded like a Russian imprecation came from the adjoining seat as the Russian climbed in. It was good to know that there was still satisfaction to be gained from the little things in life, like recycled garlic soup.

'Hold very tight, *Monsieur*,' whispered the operator. Once again Monsieur Pamplemousse had a fleeting feeling of *deja vu*. Somewhere in his early twenties, the operator was sweating profusely. His hands were trembling as he tried to engage the tongue of a 5 point safety belt.

Monsieur Pamplemousse decided on the direct approach towards his companion while he was being attended to.

'What do you know of the man who was washed up at the hotel the other night?'

He was rewarded with a non-committal shrug. 'In Russia we have a proverb: "A mouthful of sea-water gives you the taste of the ocean."'

'Meaning?'

'Meaning some people become greedy.'

'Perhaps he simply believed in free enterprise…'

'My friend, the only free cheese is in the mouse-trap.'

'We in the West would say you should never commit yourself to a cheese without first examining it,' replied Monsieur Pamplemousse, not to be outdone.

'If you are a mouse,' said the man, 'that is almost always the last thing you say. Unless you want to end up looking like a Swiss Gruyere, you'll tell me what's happened to the girl.'

Monsieur Pamplemousse stared at him. So that was it. He doubted if he had been coerced into taking a ride on the Human Slingshot simply to indulge in an exchange of national proverbs. He was about to seek final refuge by quoting Bertold Brecht – wondering out loud what happened to the hole when the cheese was no longer there, when there was a sudden whip-like crack of escaping air and before he had a chance to brace himself they took off.

An experienced astronaut would have been able to quantify the effects brought on by maximum acceleration as the cage left the ground. But even if he'd had the benefit of such a luxury, it was doubtful if Monsieur Pamplemousse would have taken it in. The loss of any sense of balance as the fluid in the inner ear went haywire, coupled with the feeling of increased weight as g-forces battled to push his body in the opposite direction saw to that.

As his heart rate gathered speed, seeking to get the vital oxygen-bearing blood flowing back to his brain as quickly as possible, a feeling of nausea swept over him.

Aware of tightening stomach muscles, he thought he was about to faint.

The momentary, but no less fervent wish that he had gone without a second helping of *L'aigo-boulido* was short-lived. As the forces of gravity overcame the forces of acceleration, the cage came to a halt and began to revolve. Almost immediately there was a violent shudder and it began to twist.

Hearing a long drawn-out gasp like the howling of a wind from somewhere far below, he opened his eyes and realised the seat next to him was empty.

A split second later came a feeling of weightlessness as the cage began its descent, hurtling towards the ground at terrifying speed. Clutching the safety bar in front of him as though his life depended on it, he looked down and saw a small crowd people gathered round a huddled shape on the concrete jetty. Mercifully no one else had been involved, but from the way the man was lying he didn't fancy his chances of a quick recovery.

Monsieur Pamplemousse didn't know what he felt? Shock? Anger? Indifference?

He wondered if it was the work of Uncle Caputo, or a genuine mistake on the part of the operator. What Todd would have called "negative over-reaction". Perhaps he had been acting under orders? Either way he wouldn't fancy being in his shoes if the Russians caught up with him.

As the up and down oscillations of the cage rapidly diminished he saw there was a fresh operator waiting for him, and he remembered all too late where he had last seen his predecessor.

It had been back at the hôtel when he had tried to send his trousers to be cleaned.

It was no wonder the youth had seemed in a highly nervous state. Clearly, his travels hadn't taken him quite as far as Mr. Pickering had pictured. He was probably already making up for lost time.

Another thought struck him as the replacement helped him out of the cage. If others subscribed to the theory of there being a third solution to every problem, he knew who would be next in line to get the blame.

In most peoples' eyes it would be a clear case of "Did the man fall, or was he pushed?"

The peril from without

'Who on earth can have sent them?' exclaimed Madame Pamplemousse. 'They must have cost a fortune.'

A *croissant* poised half-way to her mouth, she gazed at an enormous bunch of white lilies which had been delivered along with their breakfast tray. 'Are you sure there's no message?'

Monsieur Pamplemousse took a closer look. 'Quite sure.'

In total there must have been thirty long stems; far too many for the vase in their room. They looked more suited to one of the boats moored in the nearby harbour, most of which were little more than floating florist's shops anyway, and he wondered if they had been sent to the hotel by mistake. Perhaps, even now, another richer, but temporarily flowerless yacht-owner was pacing his deck working himself up into a lather.

'It could be a present from Monsieur and Madame Leclercq.'

'For what? We haven't done anything yet.'

'They don't know that,' persisted Doucette. 'You must find out. Otherwise I shan't know who to thank and that will be terrible.'

The implied division of duties didn't pass unnoticed. Stifling a sigh, Monsieur Pamplemousse picked up his cup and saucer. Watched by some anxious sparrows, he balanced a half-eaten *pain au sucre* on the rim of the cup and disappeared into the bedroom. Picking up the house phone, he dialled 5 for reception. Clearly there would be no peace until the mystery had been solved. In the meantime his coffee was getting cold.

The concierge was desolate. 'No, Monsieur, there was no message.' But he remembered the name on the side of the delivery van because it had arrived unusually early. Just as he was coming on duty, in fact. It was a well-known florist in Nice. 'If *Monsieur* would wait one moment, he would look up their number...'

Monsieur took advantage of the pause to drain his cup.

'I have it for you, *Monsieur*. If you wish, I will dial it for you and have the call transferred to your room.'

'Even better,' said Monsieur Pamplemousse, mindful of Madame Grante's current purge on the use of hotel telephones, 'give me the number and I will use my mobile.'

That apart, he wanted to get the matter settled as quickly as possible. What with one thing and another – first the body in the sea, then the episode at the fair – he had enough things on his mind without adding any more to the list.

Removing his handset from the charger, he dialled the number and waited.

When he finally got through, the girl sounded breathless. He wasn't surprised. It was early in the day and most of the staff were probably busy assembling orders. They wouldn't exactly be fighting each other to answer the telephone.

Having apologised, he explained the problem and asked for the name of the mysterious benefactor.

'I am afraid I am unable to give it to you, *Monsieur*.'

'You mean you do not have it? Surely there must be a record of it somewhere? Can you not try looking in your order book?'

'No, *Monsieur*, that is not the problem. I have the information here in front of me. It is on the computer screen.'

'Good,' said Monsieur Pamplemousse. 'Then may I have it, please.'

'That is the problem, *Monsieur*. It is because it is on the computer screen that I am unable to give it to you.'

Monsieur Pamplemousse stared at the receiver. '*Excusez-moi*. Would you mind repeating that? I do not understand.'

'I am unable to provide you with the information you require,' said the girl, enunciating the words carefully, as though addressing a hapless two-year old, 'because it would be against the Data Protection Act. How do I know you are who you say you are?'

Monsieur Pamplemousse stared at the telephone. It was happening again; a hideous variation on the list of buttons to press syndrome. Where would it all end?

'How do I know I am who I say I am?' he repeated. He was beginning to wonder himself.

'Have I the misfortune to be speaking to a distant relation of a Monsieur Kafka, late of Prague?' he demanded. 'A third cousin twice removed perhaps? I know I am who I say I am because I looked at my reflection in the mirror when I was shaving this morning. You will have to take my word for it. How do I know you are who you say you are? *Par exemple*, you could be someone from the electricity company.'

His sarcasm fell on stony ground.

'If you wish to know,' said the girl primly, 'my name is Anne-Marie and I have my instructions. It is more than my job is worth to reveal the information you are asking for. I suggest if *Monsieur* is unhappy he refuses to accept delivery.'

'That is not possible,' said Monsieur Pamplemousse. 'Your van has already been and gone. However, if you really wish to see how unhappy I am, I will catch the next train into Nice. While I am with you I will demonstrate in the clearest possible manner how much your own data storage system is in need of protection. I trust you keep it locked in a fire-proof safe.'

There was a moment's silence. 'If you were to give me some possible names of people who might be sending you flowers, *Monsieur*,' said the girl, 'I can tell you whether or not you are correct.'

Swallowing his pride, Monsieur Pamplemousse tried out Doucette's suggestions;

Le Guide, followed by Monsieur and Madame Leclercq. It sounded pathetically short.

'How about the Pickerings?' called Doucette from the balcony. 'It could be a "thank you" for dinner the other evening.'

Monsieur Pamplemousse doubted it. Including delivery charges, the flowers must have cost more than the meal, but it was worth a try.

'*Monsieur* is very cold,' said the girl. 'Perhaps you could try giving me some areas and I will tell you if you are getting warm.'

'Antibes?' said Monsieur Pamplemousse lamely, his memory for place names momentarily deserting him.

'*Monsieur* is getting warm,' said the girl excitedly. '*Very* warm...'

A thought struck him. 'If I were to mention the Hôtel au Soleil d'Or...'

'*Monsieur* is in great danger of burning himself...' The girl's voice went up an octave or two. From the sound of her heavy breathing she was almost wetting her *culottes* with excitement.

'Why didn't you say that in the first place?' he growled. 'I know. Don't tell me. You have your instructions. But when you have a spare moment, please ask your superior who is protecting who from what and from whom? Now, since I have guessed the location correctly, perhaps you can give me the name. If it wasn't Pickering, then who was it?'

'Putin,' whispered the girl. 'A Monsieur Vladimir Putin. And he paid cash. He said he was expecting a funeral. That is why they had to be all white. He seemed very cheerful about it...'

Monsieur Pamplemousse terminated the call.

'Aristide,' said Doucette, as he returned to the balcony. 'Is anything the matter? You look quite pale. Just as you were beginning to get a tan.'

'Nothing is the matter with me, Couscous,' growled Monsieur Pamplemousse. 'It is the world. It is going crazier by the minute. You are absolutely right in what you say. People have so many different ways of talking to each other nowadays, they are in grave danger of ending up barely communicating at all. When I think back to my old mother and the time when we had our first telephone...life was simple then. If it rang before nine in the morning or after six o'clock in the evening she had palpitations because it meant bad news. She was usually right. I well remember the night *Tante* Hortense fell down a well and got stuck...

'As for mobile phones...this one has brought me nothing but trouble ever since I had it.' He thrust his arm up in the air. 'That is what I think of mobile phones!'

The fluttering of wings as the sparrows perched on the balustrade hastily dispersed was punctuated by a faint splash.

'Aristide!' Doucette looked at him in horror. 'What will Madame Grante say?'

'Quite frankly,' said Monsieur Pamplemousse lamely, 'I don't care!'

The truth of the matter was he hadn't intended to let go of the mobile. It was simply that his encounter with the girl in the flower shop had made his hands sweaty, and that, in turn, had acted as a lubricant, causing the instrument to shoot from his grasp with all the velocity of a cork from a champagne bottle when it has been kept overlong in a freezer. He couldn't have done it again if he'd been paid. His heart sank as he pictured trying to explain it in a P37B.

'Perhaps I could send Madame Grante the flowers,' he said. 'Monsieur Leclercq did suggest it might be a good idea.'

'Certainly not!' said Doucette. Glancing over the balcony, Monsieur Pamplemousse's gaze softened as he saw Pommes Frites emerging from the sea. Gazing upwards as he shook off the excess water, he spotted his master. Unable to give voice to his feelings by virtue of the fact that his mouth was full, he began jumping up and down, wagging his tail with unalloyed pleasure. Love was unmistakably written large on his countenance. Clearly he was all set for an action replay.

Monsieur Pamplemousse quickly polished off the remains of his breakfast. 'I must go, Couscous,' he said. Feeling in his pocket, he produced the egg. 'The sooner I establish whether or not this rightfully belongs to Monsieur and Madame Leclercq, the sooner we can be together and enjoy what is left of our holiday.'

Madame Pamplemousse knew better than to ask him how he planned to go about doing that, and truth to tell, even if she had he couldn't have told her. As he made his way downstairs he wasn't sure where to start. At the beginning was how he had always been taught. The old electrician's formula of "assuming all external connections are correct".

The first person he met was Mr. Pickering. He was sitting on the terrace doing a crossword. An open copy of *Nice Matin* lay on the table beside him.

'I see you had a narrow squeak yesterday afternoon,' he said. 'Fame at last!'

Monsieur Pamplemousse picked up the French paper and stared at a picture of himself being helped out of the cage at the fairground. During his time with the Paris Sûreté he'd had his share of exposure in the press, usually showing him arriving at the scene of a crime, but this was the kind of publicity he could well do without. Someone must be congratulating themselves on having captured the moment for posterity.

He skimmed through the story. The police were still trying to discover the identity of the person who had occupied the seat next to him. Still trying, or didn't want to say. The search was also on for the missing operator, who was said to be English.

'Not a nice experience,' said Mr. Pickering. 'I feel partly responsible, having suggested you visit the fair in the first place.'

Monsieur Pamplemousse shrugged. 'Accidents happen.'

'According to the makers that is not possible, but then of course they would say that. However, be that as it may, it ties in with a conversation I overheard last night in the lift.

'People usually go very quiet in lifts. There isn't time to tell a long story, and if they are only going a short distance they spend the time racking their brains trying to think up something witty that doesn't need a reply. The only exception is if they think they are among foreigners who won't understand what they are saying.'

Monsieur Pamplemousse was reminded of the two Englishmen in the train.

'Last night Jan and I shared the lift with our friend – the one you aptly call Kruschev – and someone I hadn't seen before. From his accent I suspect he was from somewhere north of the Urals. They were talking about what had happened at the fair.

'It rang a bell when I saw your picture this morning. I think they may have had you in mind.'

'You speak Russian?' Monsieur Pamplemousse suddenly felt inadequate.

'Enough to recognise a serious statement when I hear one. As with Pommes Frites, certain key words cause an immediate reaction. Words like *Frantsús* – meaning Frenchman – entered the conversation. The consensus of opinion seemed to be that a *Frantsús* had to be taken care of. I'm not sure when or how, but from the way they nudged each other as we went past your floor – I couldn't help thinking of you. As I say, we didn't go far. But the little I overheard didn't sound encouraging.'

'I am planning to go into Nice this morning,' said Monsieur Pamplemousse.

'On the trail of the golden egg?'

'That is one thing,' said Monsieur Pamplemousse. 'There are other matters that need looking in to. Things to do with France.'

Mr. Pickering nodded. 'As ever, the redoubtable Miss Stein summed it up. "It isn't so much what France gives you as what it doesn't take away". Such things are very precious. It would be a pity to lose them. Are you going alone?'

'Doucette is visiting the butterfly centre with your wife.

She has been told to wear something bright and to go early, before it gets too crowded.'

'And while many of the inhabitants are still around,' said Mr. Pickering. 'Genetically modified crops and pesticides are creating havoc with caterpillars. When I was small, I had an uncle who collected butterflies. He had cases full of them, impaled in neat rows, all with grand names: Red Admirals, Purple Emperors, Silver Studded Blues.

'Nowadays you are lucky if you catch sight of a common or garden Meadow Brown.

'It is a strange life, being a butterfly. To be born so beautiful and remain that way for the whole of your life. Many ladies would pay a king's ransom for that. But as always there is a price to pay. Their average life expectancy is only three weeks.'

'What are you saying?'

'Life is very precious. I suggest you keep a close eye on what's going on behind you from now on.'

'Even better,' said Monsieur Pamplemousse. 'I am taking Pommes Frites.'

Mr. Pickering hesitated. 'You place great trust in him.'

'I would trust Pommes Frites with my life,' said Monsieur Pamplemousse simply. 'And I am sure he feels exactly the same way about me.'

'Let us hope neither of you are put to the test,' said Mr. Pickering. 'Changing the subject completely. Have you heard about the *Visiobulle*?'

'The strange-looking yellow boat with *Vision Sous-Marine* painted on the side? I have seen it around but there never seems to be anyone on it.'

'That's because the passengers are all inside the hull viewing the ocean bed through windows. They got more than they'd bargained for yesterday.

'Todd was in Juan when it arrived back, and according to him the passengers looked distinctly green about the gills when they disembarked. Apparently they had been admiring the view down below when, in amongst the flora and fauna, the posidonia plants, the sea slugs and the cucumbers, they came across a large grouper enjoying a hearty breakfast. It could well have been the remains of our friend who was washed up the other evening. The bits and pieces had been weighed down with blocks of concrete and were waving about on the ocean bed. Not a pretty sight, I imagine.

'Todd feels that once word gets around there will be a lot of fish going begging in the local restaurants. Grouper will definitely be off the menu for a while.

'On the other side of the coin, the *Visiobulle* is now doing a roaring trade running special excursions to the scene of the crime. One might almost say they are packing them in like sardines.'

'There's no accounting for human nature,' said Monsieur Pamplemousse.

'Talking of which,' said Mr. Pickering, 'how was the fish soup? It sounds as though it worked.'

'*Absolument!*' Monsieur Pamplemousse had totally forgotten his temporary loss of voice. 'The *Madame* should market it as a cure-all. She could make her fortune.'

Reaching into his pocket he took out his silent dog whistle and placed it to his lips. Moments later Pommes Frites came bounding up the steps leading to the beach. He was carrying the mobile phone in his mouth. Monsieur Pamplemousse took it from him, slipped it into his trouser pocket alongside the lap-top, and gave him a pat.

'It's all systems go then,' said Mr. Pickering. '*Bonne journée!*'

'*Merci.* And you?'

'I shall finish my crossword first. If I don't, today's papers will be in and I shall be tempted to look at the answers. After that, I think I may go for a quiet walk. Englishmen like nothing better than to disappear from time to time. The feeling that no one else in the world knows where you are is a great luxury.'

As Monsieur Pamplemousse and Pommes Frites disappeared into the hotel foyer, Mr. Pickering hesitated for a moment, then opened his guidebook. He seemed relieved by what he saw, although his satisfaction was short-lived.

Following the others out of the hotel a few moments later, he gave a frown. The parking area was almost empty. Opening the guidebook again, he examined it more closely and gave vent to an oath that might well have proved unfamiliar even to Monsieur Pamplemousse's ears. Turning on his heels, he hurried back into the hotel and ran up the stairs two at a time.

None of which failed to escape the notice of the concierge, but then concierges the world over are trained to notice such things; small departures from the norm which might impinge on the smooth running of their domain, and to act on them or not as they see fit. As such times information often went to the highest bidder.

In this particular instance the concierge of the Hôtel au Soleil d'Or simply picked up the nearest telephone and dialled a number.

Back in his room, Mr. Pickering made for the bathroom, plugged one end of a lead into the shaver socket, and connected the other to his guidebook. As soon as a red light came on he, too, picked up a telephone. His call was answered almost immediately.

'The Mercedes has gone. Probably heading for Nice, but I can't be sure. I've lost it for the time being.'

'Shitsky!'

'Exactly. There's no other word for it!'

Unaware of the ripples he had set in motion when he left the hotel, Monsieur Pamplemousse made his way up the winding road leading to the summit of the Parc du Château; a reversal of the route he had followed on his previous visit to Nice.

Taking a left fork near the top, he headed towards the

Terrace Frederick Nietzsche. Mr. Pickering was right. There were moments when being alone was a great luxury, and he felt in need of time and space in which to think. The area where the *table d'orientation* was situated sounded as good a place as any.

It was where the great 19th century philosopher had gone in search of peace and quiet during the latter part of his life. Having been brought up in a house with five women he had probably become something of an expert in such matters.

At which point Monsieur Pamplemousse's heart sank as he rounded the bend and narrowly missed being struck down by a trainload of tourists heading downhill. Emerging from behind a souvenir stand – *"Anges Plastiques* (Plastic Angels) 30fr", *"Sacs à Sacs* (Fabric sausages for storing carrier bags) 12fr" – his nostrils were assailed by the smell of cooking oil from another stand. He was one hundred and twenty years too late.

Following hard on the heels of his master, Pommes Frites took a quick look over the balustrade and stepped down again. He wasn't deeply into views. Five or six seconds was usually more than enough to tell him all he needed to know. Besides, he had other ideas and his tongue was already hanging out at the thought.

He'd caught a tantalising glimpse of the waterfall on the way up, and had he been writing a book about Nice – a kind of rough guide for *chiens* visiting it for the first time and feeling thirsty after a hard climb, it would have been in line for five stars. Better than any restaurant, and you didn't even need to be on your best behaviour.

Human beings did their best, but often they had no idea.

The walk from the station was a case in point. Coming across a sandpit with a post bearing a drawing of a dog obeying the call of nature, he had seized the opportunity to do likewise. And what had happened? A *gendarme* had blown his whistle! How was he to know he was meant to do it in the sand and not on the post?

Recognising that his master needed to be alone with his thoughts, Pommes Frites took advantage of the moment.

Briefly registering his departure, Monsieur Pamplemousse sought the shade of a nearby tree and stood for a moment gazing at the scene below. The Promenade des Anglais was crowded with match-stick figures taking a morning stroll. Here and there faster ones on roller blades, peaked caps back to front, elbows and knees padded like baseball players, were weaving their way in and out of them.

A second miniature train headed towards the Albert Gardens. Or perhaps it was the first one making good progress, for it seemed to be faring better than the lemming-like stream of traffic coming and going on either side of the palm trees in the central reservation. It was all a very far cry from the day in 1927 when Isadora Duncan had met her death when the scarf she was wearing became entangled with the wheel of her open Bugatti.

He gazed out to sea, the tiny waves sparkling in the morning sunshine. Heads dotted the water nearer the shore, and everywhere he looked there were splashes of blue; from towels spread out on the grey pebbled beach, from banners and parasols belonging to private beaches and cafés, and from chairs dotted along the promenade. To his right, beyond the red roofs of the old town, long since burnt a deep shade of ochre by the sun, the huge dome of the Negresco Hotel, a monument to "Belle Epoque", rose like a minaret above the white buildings on either side.

Looking along the coast towards Antibes he thought of Doucette and wondered how she and Mrs. Pickering were getting on with the butterflies. His thoughts then moved further on towards the school. Closing his eyes brought back memories of the music mistress conducting "Gee, Officer Krupke!". Screwing them up tighter still, holding his hands across the lids to keep out the light, the gently curving line of the Bay of Angels merged into a vision of her bending over him, mouth slightly parted as she prepared to administer the kiss of life. The moment their lips met he felt a change take place, almost as though she were struggling against some inner compulsion. For the moment at least the others gathered around them were totally forgotten. The involuntary sigh he gave vent to as she went limp in his arms came out as rather more of a groan than he had intended; certainly much louder.

'*Monsieur*... Are you unvell?'

A voice near at hand made him jump. Peering through a gap in his fingers he saw an elderly woman staring at him through pebble glasses, as though he were some kind of specimen she was about to net.

'It is nothing... a little dizziness, that is all. *Le soleil.*' Taking out a handkerchief, he dabbed at his forehead and tried out his German. '*In der sonne.*'

'*Ya? Der sonnenstich*... the strokink of ze sun...' Wherever she was from, it certainly wasn't Germany. *And* she had what looked suspiciously like five o'clock shadow!

She was about to reach into a large leather bag when a sound not unlike someone shaking a rug came from somewhere nearby. Changing her mind she turned abruptly on her heels and left. A moment later Pommes Frites appeared, looking refreshed after his bathe. He gazed enquiringly at his master.

Taking the hint, Monsieur Pamplemousse turned away from the balcony and headed towards the orientation table. Pommes Frites was right. It was a time for dealing with realities, not fantasies.

The reality was that where he was standing four hundred thousand years of history lay spread out around him. In 400BC the Greeks had named it Nikêa, and when the Romans took over some two hundred and fifty years later, forming the province of Alpes-Maritimes with Nice as its capital, they had built the town of Cimiez on the surrounding hills, where one wonderful summer's evening not so many years ago he had listened to Dizzie Gillespie playing.

In its time Nice had been fought over by Ligurians, Saracens and Barbarossa's Turkish hordes, before the pendulum swung to and fro between France and Italy.

These things had shaped the *Provencals* in much the same way as countless other influences over the centuries had shaped France *profonde*. Beyond the distant line of the Alps, *Auvergnats* like himself had become different to the inhabitants of Burgundy and different again to those in Bordeaux to the west, Brittany and Normandy to the north, not to mention Alsace, with its candle-lit fairytale windows at Christmas, to the east.

It was no wonder General de Gaulle had once bemoaned the difficulty of trying to govern a nation that had 246 varieties of cheeses. How much harder it would have sounded if he'd said 36,532 communes; 96 departments; 22 regions, which was the way it had ended up. But was that not part of France's strength; its infinite variety and its dogged independence?

Much of it was reflected in the cuisine. During the comparatively short time he had been with Le Guide, he had travelled the length and breadth of the country – a "gastronomad" as Curnonsky, self-styled prince of gastronomes would have put it – and he had seen many changes. More and more, restaurants were in the hands of accountants, who knew the cost of everything and the value of nothing.

But for all that, they still cooked with butter in Paris and olive oil in Nice. Walnut oil was still *de rigueur* in the Dordogne, just as cream and cider was in Normandy.

Deep down they all owed a debt to Auguste Escoffier who had laid down the ground rules some seventy years before in *Le Guide Culinaire*, setting standards which still prevailed today, not only in France, but all over the world.

His influence had been present in the meal they had shared with the Pickerings two evenings ago; in the clarity of the *consommé*; in the way the chicken had been carefully dissected beforehand, the bone removed from the thigh, so that each and every part had been perfectly cooked.

Was it possible that all this could be destroyed by yet another invasion, this time from a totally unforeseen direction? He would be out of a job if it were. So would millions of others. It mustn't happen!

Hearing what sounded suspiciously like a sigh, he glanced down at his feet where Pommes Frites lay with his head between his front paws. Having dried out, he was wearing his martyred expression. Monsieur Pamplemousse looked at his watch. It was 11.30. Time to move on before the firing of the noonday gun sent everyone in search of food.

'Buon giorno, Signor.' It was hard to say if the waiter recognised him or not. Either way, it didn't affect the warmth of his welcome.

It was tempting to take a seat. Pommes Frites wasn't normally very keen on pasta, but it would be interesting to see what he made of it, and he would certainly enjoy some of the sauces.

In the interests of research, Monsieur Pamplemousse decided to try somewhere new. He could always pay a return visit. There were some places you just had to go back to, and the Villa d'Este was one of them.

In the end he opted for another Italian restaurant in an adjoining street. It certainly looked less crowded.

Accepting the first table in the front row, he glanced at the selection of *plats du jour* displayed on the ubiquitous metal stand to his right, and ordered *Piccata de Veau aux cèpes* for Pommes Frites and some still water. He then opted for a *risotto au safran* for himself. A *demi vin rosé* and a Pellegrino completed the order.

Curled up under the table, Pommes Frites had chosen a position where he could keep a watchful eye on comings and goings. He was particularly wary of the roller bladers, who seemed to be out in force. That was something else he would have had added to his guidebook, under a special section marked ATTENTION! Roller bladers, along with the location of some giant cactus plants he'd come across when he'd been taken short on the way to the restaurant. Care was needed if you wanted to leave your mark on a cactus.

While he was waiting, Monsieur Pamplemousse seized the opportunity to rearrange the objects about his person. The weight in his right trouser leg pocket was beginning to make him feel lop-sided. Leaving the lap-top where it was, he squeezed the mobile into an inside jacket pocket – one of those hidden away affairs, for which it was rarely possible to find a good use. Too big for a fountain pen, too small for even the tiniest of rolled-up umbrellas, it fitted the mobile like a glove. At least no thieves would be able to get their hands on it.

Settling down, he removed the egg from another trouser pocket and replaced it with the dictating machine. He gazed at the egg. More and more the ergonomics of the whole thing bothered him. If it was meant to be a present for Madame Leclercq from her Uncle Caputo, then why had his intermediary chosen to make the hand-over on what was virtually enemy territory? It not only didn't make sense, it had clearly been a last minute decision.

Monsieur Leclercq had very definitely stated the item was to be picked up in Nice. According to Doucette they had planned to do it themselves, but because of a delayed flight they had gone straight on to Paris where Chantal had a hair appointment. That, at least, certainly rang true.

It was only at the last minute, when they arrived at the hotel, that they found the venue had been changed. The concierge had the tickets ready and waiting.

His order arrived in a large copper pan. The waiter served him a generous helping, left the pan on a stand to keep warm, then returned seconds later with grated parmesan cheese and tomato purée.

Monsieur Pamplemousse tried a mouthful of the rice before mixing in the rest of the ingredients, noting with approval that it had been first sweated in a hot pan with olive oil before the chicken stock had been added, allowing the grains to open and absorb it.

While the wine was being poured Pommes Frites busied himself under the table with his plate of veal, and with a *buon appetito*, the waiter left them to it.

Monsieur Pamplemousse returned to his thoughts. So far the Director had neither asked about the hand-over, nor had he mentioned the concert. Proof, if proof were needed, that he didn't know about the change of plans. Nor, presumably, did he have any idea of the nature of the so-called "work of art".

Was the whole thing an elaborate ploy on the part of the Russians to send a message in the strongest possible terms back to Uncle Rocco? A plot which had partially back-fired because Pommes Frites had come across the egg.

Heads turned as a young girl on roller blades entered the precinct at speed pushing an elderly lady in a wheelchair. Whatever next? He'd seen everything now. Zig-zagging in and out of the petrified pedestrians, narrowly missing an open manhole on the opposite side of the precinct where some workmen were busy erecting a protective barrier, she shot past the restaurant.

It was yet another classic Cartier-Bresson situation: the girl, young, blonde, shapely; the little old lady, her face partly covered by a shawl, a blanket draped over her lap despite the heat. If only he'd had his camera with him. But how many times had he heard that said? He hadn't, and that was an end to it. The girl and her charge had disappeared as quickly as they had come.

Helping himself to some more wine, Monsieur Pamplemousse returned to his thoughts.

Was the fact that the Russian child had gone missing a swift retaliation on Uncle Rocco's part? He wouldn't put it past him.

The question was, where did he go from here? He didn't know anyone in the Police Department at Nice. Blanchet had been moved elsewhere following one of the division's periodic upheavals. Duhesme had taken early retirement and had opened a small bar in Cannes-sur-Mer, or so it was said. At a pinch he might call in and sound him out, although whether he would want to talk would be another matter. His livelihood might be on the line.

He was beginning to wonder what he was doing in Nice at all. Why not simply let things stay as they were? Part of him was feeling irked that he had been drawn into a situation over which he seemed to have no control, for no better reason than having agreed to perform a favour. Perhaps other people were right. Perhaps it was a case of once a policeman – always a policeman. He'd always been a bit of a loner, but he suddenly missed the cameraderie of his time in the *Sûreté*; the feeling of working as part of a team.

He slipped the egg back into his trouser pocket. One thing was certain. Showing it to the local police would be tantamount to never seeing it again. In short, he was on his own.

For the second time in as many minutes he was aware of heads turning, people at other tables began pointing, and out of the corner of his eye he saw the girl again. She must have made a complete circuit of the block, following exactly the same route, only faster this time. It was like viewing a speeded-up tape loop.

This time the woman in the chair was staring straight at him. As they drew near, she threw back the blanket and it suddenly clicked home. Momentarily mesmerised, he gripped the front edge of the table. The last time he had seen her had been up on the hill, only this time, instead of pebble glasses, he found himself looking into the business end of a pistol.

To most of those present, everything from that moment on appeared to happen at once, although in fact it was Pommes Frites who reacted first. A split second before the gun went off, he leapt to his feet and gave the table an almighty heave. As it shot up into the air, scattering plates, food, glasses in all directions, a stream of bullets ricocheted off the metal surface, leaving the menu sign hanging at a drunken angle.

Before any of the stunned onlookers had time to react, and in the brief moment of silence between landing on his back with a force that jarred every bone in his body and bedlam breaking out, Monsieur Pamplemousse clearly heard the sound of something rolling across the paving.

Pommes Frites heard it too. Faced with the choice of seeing to his master, chasing after the wheelchair or finding the egg, he decided on the latter. He knew from the way Monsieur Pamplemousse kept playing with it that he set great store by the present, and from the way he was already berating a passer-by it was clear he was still in one piece.

'No,' came a bellow. 'I am *not* all right! I am lying in the middle of the road because I am about to begin a one-man *manifestation* against roller bladers, little old ladies in wheelchairs who carry sub-machine guns, and *imbéciles* who ask idiot questions.'

Looking over his shoulder, Pommes Frites was just in time to see his master struggling to sit up. His face dripping tomato purée, *risotto au saffron* covering his shirt front, he looked for all the world as though he had been left disembowelled following an unfortunate encounter with Attila the Hun. It was no wonder his would-be rescuer appeared to be in a state of shock.

Pomme Frites hurried on his way towards the open manhole. Clearly his master would live to see another day.

Hearing the sound of an approaching siren and suddenly aware of a violent pain in his right leg, Monsieur Pamplemousse sank back onto the pavement. Reaching down, he discovered it was a case of cause and effect, although he hardly had time to dwell on the matter, for moments later he felt expert hands lifting him onto a stretcher.

Although in the circumstances it was a comparatively minor problem, he found himself wondering how he would explain yet another case of damaged equipment. This time it would take more than a P37B to satisfy Madame Grante.

At least he had the consolation of knowing that not only had the lap-top's metal case saved him from serious injury – perhaps even the loss of a leg, but before leaving the hotel he'd had the foresight to download its contents to Headquarters via the built-in modem.

At which point, although he was hardly aware of it at the time, he passed out.

The man from the D.G.S.E.

Monsieur Pamplemousse came round to find he was lying on a bed in a darkened room. As he slowly regained consciousness he was vaguely aware of a voice and a figure in white flitting between him and what little light there was entering through a slatted window blind. He tried calling out, but even as the words formed he heard the sound of a door being closed.

His right side was numb and he felt partially detached from the world around him. As the memory of all that had happened gradually returned he reached down in a sudden panic and was relieved to find his leg was still there; bruised, but intact. Further investigation revealed the lap-top was missing, but then so were his trousers.

As his eyes grew accustomed to the light, he tried focusing on his surroundings: a bedside table with a carafe of water and a tumbler alongside it; a picture of a snow-clad mountain on the wall facing him; a television receiver. His jacket and trousers were hanging on a portable rail alongside an upright chair. He wondered whether anything else apart from his lap-top had been removed.

Making a half-hearted attempt at sitting up, he realised he wasn't alone. There was a man occupying an armchair in a recess near the window.

'Where am I?' A hand reached up and a light came on over his bed-head, leaving the other still in shadow. 'The Hôpital St. Roch. It was the nearest to the scene of the "accident".'

'And Pommes Frites? Where is he? Is he all right?'

'Pommes Frites?' His visitor looked puzzled.

'My dog . . .'

'Ah!' A notebook materialised. 'A bloodhound. Male. Black and tan. Traces of red here and there, some fawn. Hazel eyes. Large ears. 45-50 kilos.'

Monsieur Pamplemousse nodded and immediately wished he hadn't. His head was throbbing.

'A dog answering to that description turned up soon after the ambulance took you away. He seemed upset about something. Possibly because he couldn't find you.'

'Where is he now?' There was a shrug. 'He was last seen heading towards Antibes. A call has gone out. He refuses to let anyone get near him. Not that they want to.'

The visitor held his nose between thumb and forefinger by way of explanation. 'He had been down the sewers. Not only down, it seems, but up to his neck. Why? Nobody knows.'

Monsieur Pamplemousse felt a question being directed at him, but he didn't rise to the bait.

The man removed a small leather notecase from an inside pocket and flipped it open. 'In case you are wondering, allow me to introduce myself. Commandant André Rossetti – Direction Général de la Sécurité Extérieure.'

The surname explained the man's swarthy appearance, but as he absorbed the information Monsieur Pamplemousse wondered what a member of the French Intelligence was doing in his room. Come to that, why was he in a private room rather than a ward? He realised now why his visitor looked familiar. His face was beginning to haunt him. It belonged to the man he had first seen having breakfast with the Russian at the beach café, and later that same day when he had turned up outside the antique shop.

'You are probably about to ask why I am here.'

'I presume,' said Monsieur Pamplemousse, 'that since you have told me who you are, the rest will follow.'

'*Touché*! As you are no doubt aware, there is considerable interest in the activities of our recent visitors from across the Russian border.'

'They don't exactly hide their light under a bushel.'

'True. And while they spend their money freely nobody complains too much. But when it comes to murder in broad daylight in the centre of Nice, that is a different matter.'

'There has been a murder?'

The Commandant looked at him.

'Correction. An attempted murder. But it could well have been successful.'

'I know the gun that was used,' said Monsieur Pamplemousse simply. 'I should do. I was looking straight down the barrel. It was a 9mm Stechkin Machine pistol. Set to fully automatic, at 750 rounds a minute it is barely controllable. I was probably the safest person there. The old lady firing it – if she was an old lady – may well have done herself a mischief. It is obsolete – a relic of the East German army.'

'Another time they will choose their weapon with greater care,' said Rossetti. 'What bothers me is the cold-blooded audacity of it all. Any later in the day and it would have caused mayhem. I put it to you that your life is in great danger.'

'It wouldn't be the first time,' said Monsieur Pamplemousse.

'But it could be the last.'

Monsieur Pamplemousse considered the matter. 'Why are you telling me something I already know?'

'Because…' The Commandant rose from his seat and crossed to the window. Parting the blinds with his fingers, he looked out through the gap as though carefully weighing his words.

'As you will have gathered, things are not entirely as they seem.'

'In my experience,' said Monsieur Pamplemousse drily, 'they seldom are.'

The slats rattled back into place as his visitor turned to face him. 'What I am about to say must never be repeated outside these walls. If it is, not only will my own life be worth less than a fig, which you may well feel is of small moment, but all my work will be rendered worthless too, and that I do care about.' He paused again.

'I would like to float a balloon into the air. A balloon

containing the germ of an idea which I must tell you has received approval from on high. It will serve two purposes. First, it will ensure your safe-keeping. Secondly, it will bring those who have been gunning for you out into the open. However, putting the idea into practice is another matter. It will require your co-operation.

'In fact,' there was another, longer pause. 'A certain person has been informed, and I would go so far as to say he expects it of you.'

'Never is a very long time,' said Monsieur Pamplemousse. ' But you have my word that for the time being at least I shall keep silent.'

'Good!' The Commandant sat down again.

'Suppose, just suppose, the attempt on your life had been successful . . . I will paint a picture for you.'

Monsieur Pamplemousse lay back, closed his eyes and listened. Much of what he heard was as he had begun to suspect, although the balloon, as such, was far from what he'd had in mind.

At the end of it all he lay deep in thought, weighing the pros and cons.

'I will agree,' he said at last. 'But on one condition. My wife must be told the full story.'

Rossetti considered his response for all of five seconds. 'I can live with that,' he said.

In the circumstances, considering what he was being asked to do, and given the fact that his own life was being placed in considerable danger, Monsieur Pamplemousse couldn't help thinking the response could have been better phrased.

It was after one o'clock in the morning before Pommes Frites made it back to the Hôtel au Soleil d'Or. It had taken him much longer than he had expected on account of the time he'd had to spend dodging people in uniform who were clearly out to catch him.

The illuminated sign over the entrance had long since

been switched off and the front of the building was in darkness, so he made his way round to the back via a short cut he knew.

Having deposited his booty in the kennel, he then helped himself liberally from the water bowl, partly because the long trek had left him feeling thirsty, but also because he needed something to take away the taste. Climbing the concrete steps leading up to the terrace, he hurried past the bar where the light was still on and searched around until he found a half open service door leading into the hotel. Once inside he quickly found his way through to the reception area.

Almost immediately the sound of a gong rang out, echoing round the corridors of the hotel. Lights began to come on. The assistant concierge appeared, gave a double take, headed towards Pommes Frites, then thought better of it. Retreating behind the counter, he contented himself with a few desultory claps and some half-hearted shooing. A dog had to do what a dog had to do, and Pommes Frites clearly didn't intend leaving his post until he had received satisfaction.

Four floors up, recognising the unmistakably rhythm of a tail being used to great effect, a repeat of the sound he had heard the evening of the Pamplemousse's arrival, Mr. Pickering reached for the bedside telephone and dialled a number. A light came on in the Airstream trailer further along the road and after a brief conversation he started to dress.

'Don't forget your umbrella, dear,' said Mrs. Pickering sleepily, as he made for the door.

Monsieur Pamplemousse pushed against the lid of the coffin and peered out through the gap. A long line of black limousines stretched out as far as he could see. Not for the first time he regretted the loss of his lap-top. It would have made a unique composition. Rossetti was right about one thing. It was a no-expense-spared operation.

He hoped he was right about some of the other things he'd said too.

"There is only one thing the Mafia love better than a good murder – that is a good funeral. They will be out in force."

In vain had he pointed out that they were dealing with the Russian Mafiya, who might have a different attitude to such things. Rossetti was not to be deflected.

'It will be like the great gathering of the La Cosa Nostra in the U.S. all over again.

'Remember the 1957 meeting of top brass in Apalachin, upstate New York? Everyone turned up, from Vito Genovese and Carlo Gambino downwards. There were 58 arrests. The only one who escaped capture was Sam Giancano. But this time, instead of making arrests we will simply have our men everywhere taking pictures.'

If Monsieur Pamplemousse remembered correctly, there had been talk afterwards about the whole thing being a great betrayal. The finger of suspicion had pointed towards those members of the hierarchy, the Godfathers and the Dons, who hadn't turned up at the conference; people like Meyer Lansky, Frank Costello and Lucky Luciano.

He had to admit that so far everything had gone according to plan. When it came to funerals, Nice, with its annual death rate of nearly six thousand retirees, was a favourite catchment area for the industry. It was big business. When a person died a lot of palm-greasing went on for custody of the body.

The ergonomics of transferring of his own "body", first to the morgue and from there to the funeral parlour couldn't have been easy to arrange. A good deal of money must have changed hands to make certain people kept their mouths shut. Money, or perhaps threats – if there were handsome profits to be made there was every likelihood the Mafia would be involved somewhere along the line. That was without counting the cost of the funeral cortege itself. Presumably the coffin would be reusable – the holes bored in the side to permit the passage of air could be plugged, but there were the bearers, not to mention the hearse and all the other trappings, the flowers...

That was another thing that irked him! At the back of the funeral parlour, before he had been placed in the coffin, he had caught sight of the flowers on display; among them some from Le Guide.

He couldn't help feeling that a bunch of mixed blooms wrapped in cellophane and labelled Produce of Holland was, to say the least, minimal.

And in Nice of all places! A city famous for its flower market and its annual Festival. He couldn't read the inscription on the card, but since it clearly had Le Guide's logo at the top, he detected the iron hand of Madame Grante at work.

Alongside them, by contrast – and it was rubbing salt into the wound – there was a boxing ring complete with gloves made entirely out of flowers for a pugilist he had never even heard of. Someone else – presumably a local tippler of note – had an arrangement depicting a bottle of Hermitage vin rouge awaiting his departure. It was the size of a Nebuchadnezzar!

The least he might have expected from Le Guide was something in the shape of its logo – two escargots rampant. A couple of snails laid out on their sides would have been better than nothing and certainly wouldn't have stretched the imagination of the florist.

Raising the lid a fraction more he saw Doucette arriving. Dressed in black, she looked pale and drawn as she was helped into the first of the cars. He wanted to call out, or at least extend a finger or two, but clearly she had her mind on other things. She was accompanied by Mr. and Mrs. Pickering. The former, looking suitably funereal, was carrying the inevitable Baedeker and rolled umbrella. Pommes Frites appeared wearing a black bow round his left foreleg. That must have been Doucette's idea. He looked ill at ease, and by what was clearly popular consent he was given a car to himself. The driver was the only one who looked less than happy as he held the door open for him. There was no sign of Commandant Rossetti, but then he was probably keeping a low profile, overseeing things at the cemetery.

Catching sight of a uniformed attendant heading his way, Monsieur Pamplemousse hastily lowered the lid. The man was carrying a bucket filled with rose petals, presumably to sprinkle over his coffin, as was the custom. It was yet another of the optional extras.

Hearing voices and feeling a slight movement of the hearse as others began climbing aboard, he made himself as comfortable as possible. One half of him was beginning to wish he'd accepted the offer of a mild sedative for the journey. When he'd been asked how he was in confined spaces he hadn't realised the interior of a coffin would be quite so claustrophobic once the lid was on. At least there was no need to keep quiet. The soft lining absorbed any sound.

Apart from the flowers, it hadn't been a bad send-off. So far . . .

They set off at a slow, but steady rate. The plan was that soon after the start the hearse carrying Monsieur Pamplemousse would peel off, to be replaced almost immediately by another carrying an identical, suitably weighted coffin. After which he would be whisked away to an unspecified rendezvous where he could "disappear" for the time being.

At least he had his mobile with him, switched on at all times in case anything went wrong and he needed to be contacted – or vice versa if it came to that.

They hadn't gone far when he sensed a sudden increase in acceleration.

Instinctively bracing himself as the hearse swerved to the right, he felt the blood rush to his head as it appeared to swoop downwards, probably into a tunnel. Then gradually the dizziness passed as they began to climb and the feeling of weight transferred itself to his feet. He could still feel the speed and guessed the changeover must have happened. Probably the second car would have been waiting at the top ready to drop into place and take over at the head the procession. With luck, no one would have noticed the slight glitch.

He wondered if he should test the system and try phoning

Commandant Rossetti. Worming his arm up so that he could reach inside his jacket pocket he managed to retrieve the mobile and was about to reach for the button when he paused. The number he needed was written on a piece of paper and even if he found it there was no way he could possibly read it in the dark. That was something else that hadn't been thought through. The need to bring a torch.

He was about to return the phone to his pocket when he nearly jumped out of his skin as it suddenly began to ring.

'Bonjour, Monsieur.'

He didn't recognise the voice.

'Comment ca va?'

'Ca va,' said Monsieur Pamplemousse non-committally.

'Bon.' The voice went into what was clearly a much-rehearsed spiel, leaving no room for interruption.

Monsieur Pamplemousse stood it for as long as he could, then he took a deep breath.

'I am attending a funeral,' he barked.

It did the trick. 'I hope it is not someone close, Monsieur.' The man sounded mortified.

'Very close,' said Monsieur Pamplemousse. 'In fact,' feeling for the "off" button, he spent the few moments before pressing it describing as succinctly as possible how close it really was and why the man was wasting his time trying to sell him double glazing. It produced a very satisfactory silence.

Letting go of the phone, he gathered his strength and pushed upwards. To hell with Commandant Rossetti and his brainwaves.

Suddenly, despite the growing heat, he broke into a cold sweat. It felt as though someone had literally run an icy finger down the length of his spine. His stomach turned to water. For whatever reason, no matter how hard he pushed, the lid wouldn't budge.

For a brief moment he wondered if by chance someone was sitting on it, then dismissed the idea. It was much heavier than that. Racking his brains, he tried to remember how coffin lids were normally fastened. The inescapable truth was that it felt as though it had been screwed into place.

Despite everything, a feeling of panic began to set in. There flashed before his eyes the memory of a story that had been going the rounds when he first joined the force.

It concerned a con-man who called himself the Marquis de Champaubert. As part of a scam he had dreamed up, armed with enough food and drink for the night, and with a breathing tube connecting his coffin to the outside world, he allowed himself to be buried in a wood just outside Paris. Sadly, when the Police were called to his rescue the next morning, he was found to be dead; asphyxiated by the fumes from his own breath. He had struggled so much in trying to escape from his living tomb his clothes were torn to shreds.

It had all happened in 1929, long before he had joined the force, and doubtless the story had been embroidered over the years, but he had no wish to put it to the test or to risk having history repeat itself.

The holes in his own coffin were minuscule by comparison and already the air was beginning to foul up.

In an effort to conserve what little of it remained, he lay very still, trying to concentrate on what was happening outside in the hope of getting his bearings. But apart from the fact that while for most of the time they appeared to be driving fast through level country, every now then they slowed down or stopped altogether, suggesting they were in a built up area – it was a hopeless task. He could be anywhere.

Feeling around for the mobile, he regretted letting go of it. At some stage it must have slid out of reach. He had no idea where to look. Any thoughts of finding it and dialling 17 for the emergency services – which he could have done by feel – went by the board.

That something had gone dramatically wrong with Rossetti's plan was patently obvious. It was too late for regrets. He was on his own.

Visions of being cremated... interred alive... or even buried at sea entered his mind; nightmare scenarios that didn't bear dwelling on, except he couldn't help himself. Cremation might be the quickest way to go. Being buried at sea would be the longest. He pictured the remains of the man who had been washed up on their first night and immediately wished he hadn't.

Gradually, through the dreamlike mist beginning to envelop him, he thought he detected the sound of running water…

As he regained consciousness Monsieur Pamplemousse realised that he was once again in a strange room, only this time it was almost completely bare. He resisted the temptation to pinch himself. It was as though he had been taking part in some kind of macabre time play; a drama in which he was forever moving on, his surroundings getting bleaker and bleaker with each change of scene. It was becoming too regular for his liking.

For a moment or two he lay where he was, trying to adjust to his new surroundings. The sense of relief that he was still alive was almost palpable. The only light came from a small window let into the ceiling, far too high to reach. From the angle at which it was set, he guessed he must be in a loft. There were pipes running up one wall and from somewhere overhead he could hear the steady sound of a tank filling.

Feeling overcome by the heat, he crawled across the bare floorboards towards the solitary door. Pulling himself up by the handle, it took less than a moment to confirm that it was locked. On the same side as the handle there was a small stainless steel panel let into the wall at shoulder height. It held a light switch and alongside that a calibrated knob. He tried turning the knob in a clockwise direction. There was a creak from overhead as a weather-proofing seal round the window parted, then a welcoming draft of air. For a brief moment he thought he could hear music, but it stopped almost immediately.

Taking hold of the door handle again, he lowered himself

gently to the floor. His legs still felt weak after the journey and it was marginally preferable to standing.

Hungry, thirsty, miserable; he sat where he was for a while contemplating his lot.

To say that he had been through the worst time of his life was putting it mildly. Not only had it been the worst, but also, however long it had taken in "real" time, it had felt the longest. Whoever coined the proverb "as long as a day without bread" had never been shut inside a coffin for five minutes, let alone however long it was that he had been incarcerated. His whole life seemed to have passed before him not once, but several times before he passed out.

Automatically glancing down at his wrist, he realised his watch was missing. A brief search through his jacket pockets revealed his Cross pen was no longer there, nor was his wallet. The dictating machine hidden in the inside pocket had also been taken.

He turned his trouser pockets inside out and again drew a blank.

He had been stripped of all the things he normally took for granted: credit cards, the keys to his apartment, his diary with all the phone numbers and addresses.

More than anything, he was angry with himself for allowing the whole thing to happen. Getting involved with the D.G.S.E. at all had been a mistake. It was typical of all such organisations. The left hand often didn't know what the right hand was doing, or didn't want to know. Like their abortive attempts to assassinate President Nasser, whilst at the same time he was being supported by the CIA. It was all very well for Rossetti. He could simply sit back and see what happened.

As for the unfairness of it all… it was ironic. How many times in the heady days when he had first been made an Inspector in the Paris *Sûretè* had he told his subordinates not to grumble? How many times had he not warned them that when they went out patrolling the streets of Paris they would see ample proof that life was unfair. Not just from the time you were born, but from the moment of conception, and that you had to make the best of it. How many times had he not lectured them on the impossibility of lifting the mass of 'have-nots' to the level of the 'haves'; that in a world which was growing steadily more crowded by the second, one shouldn't assume the privileged few are necessarily happier than the so-called underprivileged. On the contrary; ulcers was a complaint mostly suffered by the former.

Looking at his current surroundings, Monsieur Pamplemousse decided he had definitely entered the realm of the have-nots. The possibility that the room he was in might end up being the last place he saw was one he didn't care to dwell on.

And all for what? All for the sake of an egg, which he had lost down a drain.

He couldn't even seek solace in the dog-eared, faded photograph of Doucette he kept inside his wallet. Taken in the early days of their courtship as she was boarding a Vedette off the Place de Pont Neuf, he only looked at it once in a blue moon, but he suddenly felt lost without it. It was like being deprived of a security blanket.

He wondered about Doucette. She must be worried sick by now. Pommes Frites, too. It was a good job the Pickerings were around.

Suddenly aware of an urgent need to relieve himself, Monsieur Pamplemousse clambered unsteadily to his feet. He had no wish to end up in a pool of his own urine. It would be an ignominious end to his career. The thought galvanised him into action.

Banging on the door with both fists, he didn't really expect to get a response, nor was he disappointed at first. But when he tried again, this time using his right foot as well, he was pleasantly surprised to hear footsteps approaching up some stairs and the sound of voices. There was the rattle of a key in the lock and the door opened to reveal two men.

He stared at them. It was hard to tell what nationality they were. Mid-European? Refugees from some Balkan state? They weren't French, that was for sure. The shorter of the two could have been a prize fighter. He had cauliflower ears and a tooth-pick between his teeth. It looked permanently attached. Both were dressed in a uniform of sorts; dark blue tee shirts, jeans and well-worn gym shoes. They didn't look particularly unfriendly; simply indifferent. Any interest in him was purely academic. He wondered if they had come from the Fairground.

He tried writhing on the spot holding on to his crotch.

The taller of the two took in the mime at a glance.

'He wants to use his pecker.' He spoke reasonable English, but with a strong American accent.

The short one removed his toothpick. 'While he's still got one.' The thought seemed to strike him as funny.

The tall one nodded. 'That'll be the first thing to go when the time comes.'

It was hard to tell if they were speaking English because they assumed he wouldn't understand, or because they knew he would and it was part of a none-too subtle softening up process.

It might, of course, be yet another example of the third alternative. English might be their only common language. You never who spoke what tongue when it came to the Balkans.

Monsieur Pamplemousse decided to play dumb, hoping he might hear something useful in the process. He soon wished he hadn't.

There was brief technical discussion in minute detail as to the order in which he might lose various parts of his body, how it would be done and what would happen to them once they had been removed. Comparisons were made with similar situations in the not too distant past. The consensus of opinion was that neither of them would fancy being in his shoes; especially if he turned out to be stupid and didn't talk. In which case he was certain to lose his legs anyway. Ho! Ho! Ho! He felt the shorter of the two eyeing his shoes for size.

At least he now knew why he was being held, but that was small comfort. That he was dealing with the Mafiya was also obvious. But if it had to do with the missing child they would be unlucky; he couldn't tell them what he didn't know. Not that such a minor detail would stop them trying. And in between? Being safely dead and buried might well be a luxury he would find himself crying out for.

In normal circumstances he was confident he could face the prospect of meeting his maker without feeling too hard done by. But while he was hale and hearty, he had no desire to see a lingering death staring him in the face through no fault of his own, and he had no intention of going down without a fight.

He wondered if his present minders had a price. Even if they did, he was in no position to offer any guarantees. Besides, they would know which side their bread was buttered on, and it would be a case of the devil you knew.

He tried another mime, this time genuinely more urgent, adding a heartfelt groan for good measure. The message went home.

As they left the room the shorter of the two men stationed himself at the top of a flight of stairs ready to block any attempt at escape, while his partner hastily led the way along a short corridor.

Opening a door, he took a brief look inside. At least there was no room for more than one person at a time. Monsieur Pamplemousse waited until the man emerged, then entered, firmly pushing the door shut behind him. Apart from obeying the call of nature he was no better off. There was no bolt on the inside and the only window was a tiny one, high up and virtually out of reach without standing on the toilet. Once again, it was remotely controlled, but it was far too small to squeeze through, even if he'd felt inclined to risk it without knowing what floor he was on. All the same he tried opening it for luck.

Then, just as he was about to flush the toilet he paused. Somewhere, far below him he could hear the sound of children at play. Suddenly everything fell into place and he realised where he was.

It figured: the fortress like construction; the high-tech electrics everywhere. The realisation gave him hope. One thought swiftly followed another. Feeling inside a half-forgotten hip pocket of his trousers his fingers touched gold.

There wasn't a moment to lose. Already he could hear a restless movement in the corridor outside. Any second there would be a knock on the door. Pressing one foot against it, he lifted the lid of the cistern and checked the inside.

What he had in mind was probably a forlorn gesture; akin to being marooned on a tiny island in the Pacific and putting a message into bottle hoping someone would find it, but anything was better than nothing.

Back in the room and left to his own devices, Monsieur entered what promised at the time to be the second longest period in his life. Not that he was anxious for visitors. The measured tread of people coming up the stairs was not something he was looking forward to hearing. Deprived of any means of telling the time, he was reduced to playing a guessing game with himself. Having decided he must be in the tower block at the school, he tried getting some idea from what he calculated must be the sun's position in the sky.

It could be, of course, that with the Mafiya turning out in force they were all still in Nice.

The rescue when it came had all the hallmarks of a Special Services force storming a hijacked plane, except that no shots were fired.

There was everything else: sirens, the roar of engines, tyres screeching, shouts, a woman screaming. Then came the pounding of feet up the stairs, followed by more shouting and an exchange of oaths. There was great crash on his door and the business end of an axe broke through the centre panel. A face appeared in the gap.

'*Où est-il?*'

'Where is it?' Monsieur Pamplemousse sized up the situation in a flash. He recognised the symptoms all too clearly. The strained expression on the man's face. The wild look in his eyes. The sense that there was not a moment to lose.

'You have come to the wrong room,' he exclaimed. 'It is the door on your right at the end of the corridor!'

Time will tell

'If I had known then what I know now, Aristide,' said Monsieur Leclercq, ' I would never have sent you to Nice.'

'And if I knew then what I know now, *Monsieur*,' said Monsieur Pamplemousse, 'I might not have gone.'

Except, of course, he would have done. Anyway, the Director didn't know the half of it. He had deliberately kept his story short. Had he not done so, Monsieur Leclercq would have gone into every detail at great length and they would have been stuck in his office until Doomsday. As it was, Pommes Frites was already beginning to show signs of unrest.

He'd been right about the flowers. Doucette hadn't been the only person to be let into the secret of the scam. Word had reached Monsieur Leclercq and he in turn had passed it on to Madame Grante. It also explained the absence of any other mourners from Le Guide.

The Director picked up the egg and held it for a moment. It was a gesture Monsieur Pamplemousse had become all too familiar with. The careful weighing in the palm of the hand, followed by a closer look; then the holding of it up to the light.

'To think that someone died because of this!' Monsieur Leclercq selected a button from one of a row let into his desk and pressed it, causing a slatted blind in the south facing wall of his office on the top floor of Le Guide's headquarters in the rue Fabert to rise. Sunshine streamed in as he crossed to the window.

'Chantal must never know, of course,' he continued, holding the egg up to the light. 'She would be mortified. She loves her Uncle very dearly, but he can be over-generous at times – especially with other people's property.'

Monsieur Pamplemousse shrugged. 'If it hadn't been the

egg, *Monsieur*, it would have been something else. A painting, perhaps. A figurine.'

'If only it had the power of speech, what tales it could probably tell. Sagas involving the cream of the Russian aristocracy. Stories of love and intrigue…'

'Perhaps,' said Monsieur Pamplemousse pointedly, 'it is better for all of us that it can't talk, particularly when it comes to describing more recent events.'

The Director hastily changed the subject.

'I must say it does look in need of a polish. It is slightly encrusted with dirt here and there. On the other hand, the sunshine makes it look almost good enough to eat.'

'I wouldn't recommend it, *Monsieur*.'

Monsieur Leclercq sniffed the egg.

'You are right, Aristide. I do detect a somewhat peculiar odour, not unlike one that has gone addled. It is hard to place, but…' Pondering the problem he gazed out across the rooftops of Paris, as though seeking inspiration in the golden dome of the Hôtel des Invalides. 'Where have I come across it before?'

'With respect, *Monsieur*, I think you should set you sights a little lower,' said Monsieur Pamplemousse.

'What are you saying, Aristide?'

'The *œuf* you are holding to your nose has recently spent some time wallowing in the mire beneath the streets of Nice.'

'*Dans les egouts*?' The Director nearly dropped it at the thought. 'What, may I ask, was it doing in the sewers of the Côte d'Azure? Come to that, what were you doing down there, Pamplemousse? It is no wonder you are without a tan. Don't tell me you were testing the canteen facilities? However good they are, they are hardly likely to be on our list of recommended eating establishments. I can't picture them being worthy of a bar stool, let alone a Stock Pot, although a stool might well be an apposite symbol.'

'I doubt if the inhabitants would appreciate such an award anyway, *Monsieur*. In my experience bureaucracy is often at its worst below street level. The employees of sanitation departments seem to hold a jaundiced view of those in other walks of life. Welcome is not writ large on their faces if you happen to come across an open manhole and look down on them. Rather the reverse.'

'When you are working below ground like that, Pamplemousse,' said the Director reprovingly, 'exposed to human detritus for hours on end, I daresay it is all too easy to take a jaundiced view of the goings-on overhead, especially when it is somewhere like Nice, devoted as it is to the sybaritic pleasures of life. The contrast must be even greater than usual when you come up for air.'

'On the other hand, *Monsieur*, if they are anything like the Paris sewers, they do say that after the waters have been processed it is possible to drink them.'

'They – whoever "they" may be – can say it until they are blue in the face. I very much doubt if those in charge practise what they preach. I shall remain faithful to those waters emanating from the springs of Vichy, preferably Celestin.

'However, all that is by the by. It doesn't explain what the egg was doing down there in the first place.'

'The simple explanation, *Monsieur*, is that I had the misfortune to lose it down one of the open manholes I mentioned. It would be wrong if you were to thank me for its recovery. I was lying in the road at the time. It was entirely Pommes Frites' doing.'

'Pommes Frites!' The Director's voice softened as he turned and gazed towards a dark corner of the room where a familiar form was sitting quietly beneath a small table listening to the conversation. 'Hiding his light under a bushel as ever.'

'They do say a bloodhound can pick up a trail that is anything up to two weeks old,' said Monsieur Pamplemousse. 'On this occasion it was fresh...'

'Nevertheless,' broke in the Director, 'it was a signal achievement. He must have had a wide choice. It says a great deal for his olfactory powers that from all the scents assailing his nostrils he was able to pick up that of a single *oeuf*.'

Hand extended, the Director set off to traverse the vast expanse of carpet in order to offer his congratulations, but as he drew near Pommes Frites he seemed to think better of it and turned instead to a control panel let into the wall and turned one of the knobs.

A draft of cool air wafted across the room, ruffling Pommes Frites' fur in the process.

'*Sacré bleu*!' Monsieur Leclercq hastily turned the knob as far as it would go in the reverse direction.

Uttering cries of *"formidable!"* he retraced his steps and flung open a window. 'One thing is certain, Pamplemousse. Others will have no trouble following Pommes Frites' trail for some weeks to come.'

'I fear the smell lingers,' said Monsieur Pamplemousse. 'Notwithstanding several baths in strong disinfectant before leaving Nice, we had the carriage to ourselves on the train back to Paris.

'We met with a similar problem on the *autobus* this morning. Fortunately the number 80 was extremely crowded and we had to stand, so few people knew where the smell was coming from, but it was not a happy journey. There was a good deal of unrest: cries of *"merde!"* and *"nom d'un nom!"* mingled with shouts of "Stop the bus". Half the occupants wanted the windows open, the other half said it only made matters worse and wanted them closed. The latter won, of course. It is the rule. When there is an argument those who want it closed have priority.'

'I have never been on an *autobus*,' said the Director. 'It is another world. Perhaps,' he added thoughtfully, 'he might appreciate going through the car wash at my local garage. He could take this egg with him and kill two birds with one stone.'

'It is only a matter of time,' said Monsieur Pamplemousse. 'I am meeting my wife shortly. Doucette is of the opinion that a walk in the Luxembourg Gardens followed by a dip in the Seine will work wonders.'

'Would that I could accompany you, Aristide,' said the Director, 'but I fear I have an important meeting scheduled.'

Returning to his desk he opened a drawer. 'Changing the subject – and this will please Pommes Frites too – it so happens that I have a surprise for you both.'

Removing a small parcel he began slowly unwrapping it, milking the moment for all he was worth.

'Le Guide's issue camera has been found. It had been buried in the sand on the beach outside the Hôtel au Soleil d'Or. By sheer chance a small child who had been given a treasure seeker for her birthday came across it. She has been suitably rewarded, of course. I have sent her a signed copy of this year's guide.

'Had you gone to Le Touquet as planned, who knows what state the mechanism would have been in with the tide ebbing and flowing twice daily. Nevertheless,' he held the camera aloft, 'it is a great tribute to the manufacturing standards of Messrs Leitz. So much so, it has led me to believe we should seize the opportunity.

'I understand they recently received a lifetime award for the greatest contribution to photography of the twentieth century – the development of the 35mm Leica camera.

'There are parallels to be drawn. Our own contribution to the world of *haute cuisine* has not gone unremarked among the powers that be. What I have in mind is a joint advertising campaign extolling the old-fashioned values common to both our organisations.'

'A photograph of the camera alongside a copy of Le Guide, perhaps?' suggested Monsieur Pamplemousse. The Director's enthusiasm was infectious. He could see it all.

'That is one possibility, Aristide,' said Monsieur Leclercq, clearly gratified at the reception accorded his idea. 'However, I have since had another flash of inspiration.' Reaching across his desk, he pressed a button.

'Vèronique... Have the prints arrived? Good. Bring them in.' He turned back to Monsieur Pamplemousse. 'As it happens there was a film in the camera and I asked Trigaux to process it. If the pictures turn out well, they will lend added interest to the campaign. A film which has been inside a camera, which has itself lain buried in the sands of Cap d'Antibes for several days will be quite unique.'

Monsieur Pamplemousse looked puzzled. 'But I didn't have time to take any pictures, *Monsieur*. If you recall, I had only just finished loading a new spool when I was attacked from behind.'

'With respect, Aristide, I think you are mistaken. Trigaux assured me the film had been wound back into its cassette, so it must have been exposed. I am hoping you may have some shots of the hotel or the beach. They would be particularly apposite.'

Monsieur Pamplemousse didn't pursue the conversation, for at that moment Véronique entered the room carrying a large manila envelope. It struck him she was looking unusually nervous as she handed it to Monsieur Leclercq. Patently avoiding eye to eye contact, she left again as quickly as possible.

'And now, the moment of truth!' Lifting the unsealed flap, the Director felt inside the envelope, withdrew a handful of 210 x 297 mm enlargements, and spread them out across his desk. 'What did I tell you?' he exclaimed. 'Most satisfactory. Typical of the standard one has come to take for granted from Leica – pin-sharp images – all beautifully exposed – lovely gradations. Each one a work of art.'

Seeing that at first sight the prints appeared to be upside down, he riffled through the pile, turning them round to face the other way. As he did so Monsieur Pamplemousse managed to get a closer look. His heart sank. It was no wonder the Director's secretary had looked nervous. Taking a deep breath while he waited for the storm to break, he pictured her doing the same thing in the outer office. It had gone very quiet.

The several seconds which elapsed while Monsieur Leclercq stared at the photographs before he exploded felt like an eternity.

'What are you doing lying on the ground like that, Pamplemousse?' he demanded. 'And what are all these girls up to?' He picked up another picture. 'And why is that woman crouching over you? She looks young enough to be your daughter.'

'She was about to give me the kiss of life, *Monsieur*.'

'In the *soixante-neuf* position?'

'We all have our methods,' said Monsieur Pamplemousse defensively.

'And this one,' Monsieur Leclercq picked up a third print. 'What, may I ask, is that object you are clutching?'

'Monsieur Pamplemousse took a closer look. 'It is my baton, *Monsieur*.'

'I am not interested in what you call it, Pamplemousse,' barked the Director. 'I am more concerned with what you intend doing with it.'

Picking up a magnifying glass, he took a closer look. '*Mon dieu*! It is not possible?'

'It is kind of you to say so, *Monsieur*,' said Monsieur Pamplemousse. 'But it is not what you think. It is a *saucisson*. If you remember, I bought Pommes Frites a *Bâton de Berger* as a treat. I had been using it in order to defend myself…'

'Stop!' bellowed the Director. 'I do not wish to hear another word. 'Is there no end to your depravity? These photographs are worse than the last ones you sent me. Far worse! In the first film you were patently preparing yourself for an orgy of the very worst kind. But these defy description. What am I going to tell the Leica representative when he arrives from Dusseldorf?'

'With respect,' said Monsieur Pamplemousse, clutching at straws. 'I think he will be coming from Wetzler. That is where their main offices are.'

'Stop splitting hairs, Pamplemousse,' barked the Director. 'I have told you about it before.'

'And what was Pommes Frites doing all this time?' he continued. 'Keeping a watchful eye open I imagine? Baring his teeth to make sure no passers-by interrupted you while you satisfied your base desires.'

Monsieur Pamplemousse's face cleared. 'That was it, *Monsieur*. I remember now. He must have been taking the pictures.'

The Director's eyes bulged. 'I can hardly believe my ears!' he exclaimed. 'I thought I had heard everything, but training a dog to record your unseemly activities beggars belief. No doubt you also persuaded him to bury the camera in the sand until such time as you could retrieve the film after dark.'

'You misunderstand me, *Monsieur*. There is a very simple explanation. Pommes Frites chased after my assailant and wrestled the camera from him. When he returned he had it in his mouth and it so happened that not only was it still set to automatic, but it was pointing in my direction. One of his incisors must have made contact with the shutter release. I remember hearing a whirring noise. That was why he rushed off and buried it. He probably thought it was a bomb. It is what he is trained to do. As for the girl who was bending over me…why, Leitz could make capital of the fact that even a dog can take wonderful pictures if he owns a Leica…'

Monsieur Pamplemousse broke off. The Director was now leafing through the shots taken with the aid of the lap-top. Having glanced at the first one with a certain amount of distaste, he fastened on the second.

'You didn't tell me you had met with Chantal's Uncle,' he exclaimed.

Monsieur Pamplemousse's gazed at the picture. It was a blow-up of the one he'd taken of the two men having breakfast at the beach cafè the first morning of his stay.

'What does it all mean, Aristide?' asked Monsieur Leclercq. 'I must confess I have lost track.'

Join the club, thought Monsieur Pamplemousse. His mind was in a whirl.

'I think, *Monsieur*,' he said at last, 'it means that at the end of the day it is a case of better the devil you know, than the one you don't.'

'One last thing before you go, Pamplemousse' said Monsieur Leclercq. 'Please put me out of my misery. Why are both your thumbs in plaster?'

'It would take rather long to explain, *Monsieur*. You may remember my mentioning Doucette's problem and my interest in the art of Shiatsu . . . '

'I trust you haven't been practising it behind the dunes at the Hôtel au Soleil d'Or,' said the Director.

'There are no dunes on the beach at the Hotel au Soleil d'Or, Monsieur. The sands are like a billiard table.'

'That is even worse,' said the Director. 'I am surprised Madame Pamplemousse agreed. Presumably it took place after dark?'

'Oh, no, Monsieur. Neither did it involve Doucette.'

He picked up one of the enlargements – the group shot that had been taken at breakfast time – and pointed to a figure in the middle. 'It was this lady here.'

The Director stared at it. *'Mon Dieu!'*

'It was all in the course of duty,' said Monsieur Pamplemousse hastily. He held up two fingers resting one upon the other. 'For a time she and I were like this.'

'I trust, Aristide, that you were the one on top,' said the Director.

'Alas, no. As I discovered to my cost, she is the holder of a black belt in ju jitsu.'

'Would it be foolish of me to ask why you were treating her?'

'I think for some strange reason her husband credited me with the return of their daughter, although I suspect your wife's Uncle was more than pleased to be rid of her. However, feeling he owed me a favour, he suggested I might like to borrow his wife for the remainder of my stay.'

'Hardly a fair exchange,' said the Director, relieving Monsieur Pamplemousse of the photograph, 'but then, different cultures place different values on these things.'

'He is also easily offended,' said Monsieur Pamplemousse, 'so I could hardly say no. When I discovered she suffered with her bones in much the same way as Doucette, I made *her* an offer she couldn't refuse. Honour was satisfied on both sides.'

'It is no wonder your thumbs suffered in consequence,' exclaimed Monsieur Leclercq, making use of his magnifying glass. 'All that bombazine to penetrate.'

'In the event that wasn't necessary, *Monsieur*.'

The Director stared at him. 'I have always understood, Pamplemousse, that one of the main advantages of Shiatsu is that patients have no need to remove their clothing.'

'It was not my fault she chose to,' said Monsieur Pamplemousse. 'We had a language problem and I think she misunderstood my mime. She is a very solid lady and there was a lot of territory to cover. Following her meridians was not the easiest thing in the world. Interestingly she had a surprisingly tiny voice for her size. The response each time I came across a pressure point was quite remarkable. Were I to put a culinary value on her squeaks they would certainly merit three Stock Pots. It was a great strain maintaining the pressure in order to bring the Yin and the Yang together in harmony.'

The Director gave a shudder. 'I don't think I want to hear any more. It is no wonder you are looking peaky, Pamplemousse. Your vacation doesn't seem to have done you any good at all.'

Abruptly changing the subject, he opened a desk drawer. 'Which reminds me. I have a letter which arrived for you this morning.'

Slitting open the envelope as best he could with a damaged thumb, Monsieur Pamplemousse, withdrew a sheet of paper and scanned through it.

" ...you will be pleased to know our friends have taken the hint...scattering along the coast...Todd is trying to find somewhere to park...in Cannes of all places! In June! Who knows where they will turn up next! Jan is on her way home. There is an important meeting of the W.I. Meanwhile, I am heading for San Marino...Let's hope the weather is good and I have no need for my umbrella..."

Reading on, the last paragraph brought a smile to his lips. Glancing up he realised the Director was watching him intently.

'Forgive me, *Monsieur*. It is from an old friend I met while we were away. He is apologising for the fact that one his colleagues telephoned me at a singularly inopportune moment. He had been told to check that I was alive and well. As he had no idea what was going on he pretended to be a double-glazing salesman.'

'A double-glazing salesman!' Monsieur Leclercq's delivery could hardly have been bettered by Dame Edith Evans at her peak of her career,

He gazed at Monsieur Pamplemousse with a mixture of awe and affection. It was hard to tell which was uppermost.

'Much as I value your work for Le Guide, Aristide' he said, 'there are times when I wonder whether you shouldn't consider a career change.'

Monsieur Pamplemousse forbore to say there were times when he felt much the same way himself. Instead, he waited for the other to continue.

'On the other hand,' Monsieur Leclercq held out his hand, 'I sincerely hope you don't. Life would be very dull without both you and Pommes Frites!'

Doucette was already waiting by the entrance to the Luxembourg Gardens when they reached the Rue Auguste Comte, and together all three made their way inside via the gate Place André Honnorat.

Among the many signs attached to the ironwork was one

headed *Access des Chiens.* Pointing out that dogs were required to use either the gate they had just passed through or one in the Boulevard Saint Michel, there was a map alongside it showing exactly where they were allowed to go once they had entered, provided always that they were on a leash.

Blissfully unaware of the fact, and having signally failed to recognise anything in the accompanying symbol even remotely resembling a fellow creature, Pommes Frites sailed through the opening as to the manner born and promptly set off along a tarmac path in hot pursuit of a tiny radio-controlled motor-cycle operated by the father of a small boy.

Taking hold of Doucette's arm, Monsieur Pamplemousse pretended not to notice and led his wife along one of the parallel gravel paths.

It was all very well for Pommes Frites. Despite their long walk, he was still full of beans. Like a small child let out of school for the morning break, he was making the most of his freedom. Quickly abandoning the miniature motor cycle in favour of a stall selling coloured hoops and picture postcards, he gave it a cursory inspection, left his mark on a nearby statue, then set off at a gallop along the far side of a flower bed.

Seeing his head bobbing up and down behind vast displays of dahlias, begonias and nicotana, it struck Monsieur Pamplemousse that colourful though the scene was, it could be forbidden territory. Out of the corner of his eye he spotted two gendarmes who had clearly reached a similar conclusion.

As they set off in hot pursuit, he gently steered Doucette towards the nearside of the bed, away from the action.

Speaking personally, he was looking forward to having a sit down, but he might just as well have dreamed of going to the moon. It was Wednesday afternoon – a half day holiday for schools – and there wasn't a spare chair to be had.

Ahead of them lay the Grand Bassin, the octagonal pond which, ever since Napoleon decreed the gardens should be dedicated to children, had been reserved for model boats. If the armada of blue and white sails was anything to go by, the Emperor's wishes were being amply fulfilled that afternoon.

And all around them it seemed as though lovers, oblivious to their surroundings, were gazing into each other's eyes. The simple pleasures of life for the young at heart were all to hand. Even the pigeons seemed to have but one thing on their mind, but then they always did.

Seeing a couple locked in each other's arms reminded him of Katya.

'Why do you keep sighing, Aristide,' said Doucette. 'Is anything wrong?'

'I was thinking of something Monsieur Leclercq said to me earlier today, Couscous,' said Monsieur Pamplemousse hastily.

Abandoning his search for somewhere to sit, he paused by a flight of stone steps leading up to the wooded part of the gardens.

'I met Madame Leclercq's Uncle Caputo while we were in Nice.'

'You didn't tell me, Aristide.'

'That is exactly what the Director said. The point is, I didn't know it at the time.'

'But didn't he realise who you were?'

'Not at first. There was no reason why either of us should have recognised the other. We have never met. Probably, after he had spoken to the Director it was a different matter, but by then he chose not to let on. By Monsieur Leclercq's own admission Uncle Caputo has his fingers in many pies; most of them distinctly unsavoury.

'When he came to see me in the hospital he posed as a member of the Direction Général de la Sécurité Extériere and led me to believe that he had managed to infiltrate the Mafiya posing as a bent agent. At the time I had no reason to doubt him. Where there is big money involved there are always underhand dealings going on. The D.G.S.E. are no exception.

'In fact, he was probably trying to reach an arrangement with the Russians in order to protect his own territory, but when that began to go sour following the death of the antique dealer, he kidnapped the daughter in retaliation.

'When they took a pot shot at me and I ended up in hospital he came up with the idea of the funeral. He suggested to the Mafiya that it would be a spectacular way for them to make their mark and establish themselves in the area. In fact, he hoped it would bring as many of them out into the open as possible so that he could identify them.'

'Is that what you call spraying people with bullets, Aristide? Taking a pot shot?'

'Apart from the sign outside the restaurant, it didn't do any great damage,' said Monsieur Pamplemousse.

'I still don't understand what went wrong,' Doucette persisted. 'When the hearse suddenly took off and disappeared down an underpass I didn't know what to do. And by the time the other cars had stopped it was too late anyway.'

Monsieur Pamplemousse gave shrug. 'Unbeknown to Uncle Caputo, the Mafiya had already infiltrated some of the funeral parlours of Nice, taking over from the old Mafia. He happened to pick on the wrong one.'

'All because of an egg,' said Doucette. 'Do you think the Leclercq's will keep it?'

'I doubt it,' said Monsieur Pamplemousse. 'The Director will be much too worried about his reputation and that of Le Guide. Think of the scandal if it ever got out that he was a receiver of stolen property. Although what he will do...'

He broke off as he heard the shrill blast of a whistle coming from the direction of the Grand Bassin.

Fearing the worst, he wasn't disappointed. Looking round, he was just in time to catch sight of a shape, not unlike that of a porpoise, threshing around in the pond, scattering boats as it went. It looked like the aftermath of the Spanish Armada. The Emperor must be turning in his grave.

Conspicuous among the crowd that had gathered to watch Pommes Frites disporting himself were the two gendarmes he had seen earlier. Both were on their hands and knees trying to drag him over the edge on to dry ground.

'*Merde!*'

Emerging, not without difficulty from the green waters, Pommes Frites rewarded their efforts by shaking himself dry.

Hastily regrouping, one of the gendarmes produced a handkerchief and held it to his nose while he set about examining the tag on Pommes Frites' collar. Monsieur Pamplemousse's heart sank. The name would undoubtedly ring a bell. The second officer, the plumper of the two, began talking into her mobile.

'*Alors!*' Doucette looked on with alarm. 'It is all my fault for suggesting we come here. Perhaps if you were to pick him up, Aristide? I've seen others carrying their dogs and they seem to get away with it.'

'*Merci beaucoup,*' said Monsieur Pamplemousse gloomily, 'but I have no wish to give myself a hernia and catch my death of cold into the bargain. Besides, I fear it is already too late.'

Pommes Frites' encounter with the law had already reached the "taking down of details in a notebook stage".

'I think, Couscous, I may put plan B into action before they throw the book at us.'

Taking the steps two at a time, he paused at the top to get his breath back before producing his trusty dog whistle. Placing it to his lips, he blew as hard as he could. Although beyond the range of human hearing, it had an immediate effect.

Pricking up his ears, Pommes Frites wriggled free from his captor and to cheers from the crowd set off round the perimeter of the pond in the opposite direction from his master. Over the years he had developed a sixth sense in such matters and there was no question of him giving the game away. There followed a desultory chase, with the female gendarme giving up long before the end of the first lap and her colleague following suit shortly afterwards. Neither looked in the pink of condition.

'Hurry, Couscous.' Grabbing his wife's arm, Monsieur Pamplemousse beat a hasty retreat. By-passing the area given over to pedal-operated go-carts, skirting round the tennis courts, he stopped just short of the adventure playground – its slides, roundabouts and climbing frames positively teeming with small figures, and branched left towards the south west corner of the gardens and safety.

Over the years he had come to think of it as "Monks Corner", mostly on account of the monastic pursuits taking place there: long term projects such as bee keeping and the planting of fruit trees.

It was the part he liked best of all: a haven of peace, a sanctuary given over to the tending of some 600 different varieties of dwarf apple and pear trees. Meticulously trained on espalier frames, with labels recording the date of planting, the variety, the names of their many different shapes: simple and double U, trident, cordon, pyramid and goblet, it was a living monument to orderliness and the infinite patience of man. At this time of the year each individual fruit was painstakingly encased in a protective wrapping of plastic or paper to protect it from the birds.

He paused by a board to read once again the story of the most famous tree of all: a *Louise Bonne d'Avranche*. Planted in 1867, not long after the formation of the Third Republic, it had taken 50 years to train its 19 vertical branches to their full height. In its maturity it had yielded 100 kg of pears annually until its death in 1978 at the age of 111.

'To think, Doucette, it was just a tiny plant when the massacres of the Paris Commune took place. Since then, France has survived two World Wars, Presidents have come and gone ... undreamed of things have happened: the coming of the aeroplane, television, man landing on the moon ... '

'It is very reassuring to know that some people are still prepared to spend their days working on things they will never live to see and enjoy, simply for the benefit of their fellow man,' said Doucette.

Monsieur Pamplemousse gave her arm a squeeze.

Nice suddenly seemed far away. And yet, if Nice was anything to go by, despite wars, famine, cholera, and everything else that had been thrown at it over the centuries, the cicadas were still singing; and doubtless the olive tree outside the school would survive being struck by lightning. It took a lot to kill an olive tree. What was the old proverb?

"If you cut me do I not become more beautiful? If you uproot me, I am hurt. But only if you destroy me completely do I die." Somehow it summed it all up.

Lingering for a moment by a bronze relief map of the Luxembourg Gardens, erected for benefit of the blind, Doucette ran her fingers over the raised characters. The only sound came from the distant click of metal against metal from the nearby boules area.

'We are really very lucky.' She took one last look round the gardens as they went on their way. 'Perhaps there are parallels to be drawn, Aristide. One must always believe that in the end the good things will triumph over the bad, but patience is needed.'

'Patience,' said Monsieur Pamplemousse, 'and a belief in truth, justice and humanity. It is sometimes a lot to ask.'

Pommes Frites, another living monument to patience, was waiting for them outside the small building housing the Headquarters of the apiarists of Paris. He looked as though butter wouldn't melt in his mouth, and for once he seemed to be taking note of the warning signs, not only keeping well clear of the hives, but a nearby notice that had a picture of a bee on it.

Greetings exchanged, they beat a hasty retreat into the rue Vavin and took refuge in the first cafè they came to.

Monsieur Pamplemousse ordered a *citron pressé* for Doucette and a *pastis* for himself. He felt in need of it.

'Did you know Mr. Pickering had a tracking device hidden

in his guide book?' asked Doucette, after their order had arrived. 'He managed to attach a transmitter to the hearse. That's how he knew where they had taken you.'

'Nothing surprises me about Mr. Pickering,' said Monsieur Pamplemousse. 'It was a stroke of genius on his part to call out the *Pompiers-Sapeurs*. As I told you, Couscous, they are always there when you need them.'

'What makes you think he called them, Aristide?'

'If he didn't, then who else would have? I can't picture Todd doing it. Being in a foreign country and given the circumstances, both would have needed to tread warily. It is a question of territories.'

'I was not in a foreign country, Aristide,' said Doucette quietly.

Monsieur Pamplemousse looked up from the delicate task of adding water drop by drop to his drink.

'You!'

Doucette nodded.

'But what did you say?'

'I simply told them there was a man locked in a room at the top of the school building and that if they wanted their ball back they should get there as quickly as possible. I think they found it all rather more than they had bargained for, but it didn't stop them.'

'It takes a lot to stop *Les Sapeur-Pompiers*,' said Monsieur Pamplemousse. 'They are not called the "Soldiers of Fire" for nothing. But how did you know I was in the tower?'

'I had a telephone call from someone at the school.' said Doucette. 'She sounded desperate. Her name began with a K...'

'Katya. I must write and thank her.'

'She told me you had tied one of her handkerchiefs to something called a *flotteur*, whatever that may be.'

Sensing he was on dangerous ground, Monsieur Pamplemousse drained his glass and signalled for *l'addition*.

'It is a simple float,' he said, as they made their way down the rue Notre Dames des Champs. 'It is shaped like a ball and it shuts the water off when a cistern is full. I needed something not too heavy, just enough to stop it being blown away and perhaps land in a tree. Fortunately the one in the school's toilet was made of copper rather than plastic, so it was exactly right – it landed right in the middle of the play area. Removing it also meant that in the fullness of time water began coming out of the overflow pipe, so when the *Sapeurs-Pompiers* arrived they knew exactly where to go.'

'I understand all of that,' broke in Doucette impatiently. 'What puzzles me is how you came to have the girl's handkerchief in the first place.'

Monsieur Pamplemousse stared at her. 'Ah, now, Couscous,' he said, 'I'm glad you asked me that!' Feigning temporary deafness due to the noise from traffic in the busy boulevard Raspail, he took hold of his wife's arm again and hurried her across the road towards the Metro entrance on the central reservation.

Following close behind, Pommes Frites wore his enigmatic expression: a mixture of admiration and anticipation. He enjoyed listening to his master's stories, not so much because he knew what they were about; most of the time he didn't. But he liked seeing the effect they had on other people.

As far as he could remember there were thirteen stops between where they were and home, which meant there would be plenty of time. He hoped the train wouldn't be too crowded.

With luck there might even be a man squeezing a box and making music come out. It had happened to him once before and he had never forgotten it.

It was nice there were so many things in life to look forward to.